SPECTERS

ECHOES OF DESPAIR

BY MICHAEL EMOND

This book is dedicated to everyone out there alone in their head

*and haunted by their inner demons. ...**You are not alone.***

Memento Mori.

All living things must one day die.

Life moves on with or without you.

Seize the day or be left behind with your regrets.

We've only one life to live, so make the most of every moment.

Treasure this both terrible and wonderful gift you were bestowed.

CHAPTER 1

THE BOY HAUNTED BY HORRORS UNSEEN

I stood on a rooftop. The sky was a creamy orange, like the color of marmalade from the setting sun. A gentle breeze blew against my face as I returned to this place once more. How many times have I stood upon this rooftop now? How many times have I revisited this memory? How many times have I relived this pain and sorrow? I cannot recall.

I felt a sudden lurch in my stomach.

"Mom!" I screamed.

I opened my eyes. I was sprawled out on my couch with the sci-fi novel I was reading earlier lying open against my chest. I ended up falling asleep reading again. I still felt groggy as I stretched out my neck and my shoulders, glancing at the digital clock on my microwave, which now read 3:30.

"Son of a—" I muttered under my breath.

I had class in forty-five minutes. I didn't even have time to tame the frizz in my hair or wipe the sleepiness from my eyes. I reluctantly got off my couch, lazily trying to brush out the wrinkles in my t-shirt. I then went to grab my windbreaker, which was tossed on a chair by the kitchen counter the day before. I grabbed my apartment key, which was set on a collapsible table. I used to eat on. I grabbed my bag, which was carelessly thrown under the table as well. I made sure I took a moment to lightly clap my hands to my cheeks in a vain effort to perk myself up before finally heading out the door.

I lived in a small studio apartment. It was located in a two-story building that was set up like a cheap motel with an open terrace to access the apartments on the second floor. The space was limited, the walls were thin, my neighbors were loud, and I never had enough hot water for a shower, but this place felt far more preferable than living with my relatives. I placed my key into the door's lock, giving it a slow turn until I heard a click.

"It's your fault!" a voice cried.

I pulled out my key from the lock and was greeted by an eerie-looking thing vaguely resembling a crow as I stepped away from my door. It returned my gaze while perched on the terrace railing. Its feathers were jagged and messy, with three blood-red eyes placed seemingly at random on its skull. Just looking at it made my skin crawl. It was as if my body was instinctively recoiling at the mere sight of it.

"Ungrateful boy!" the bird shouted.

I sighed before walking away and paying it no mind. I knew from prior experience that these shadowy figures would go away on their own if I left them alone long enough. It was no use fretting over them when I had somewhere I needed to be. Suppressing my continued annoyance, I put my key in my coat pocket and made my way down the stairs.

#

I was a sophomore at Clover College, a small private school smack dab in the middle of nowhere in the Midwest. The classroom building I needed to go to today was a 15-minute walk away from my apartment. I was just glad the weather was nice today, even if it was mildly brisk for September. It could have been worse. At least it wasn't raining. My walks to campus were always quiet ones, most of the time anyway. I made my way up the faded and cracked sidewalk while the occasional car passed me by on the main road.

"Useless child!" a voice cried.

I stopped walking and looked towards a fence post across the street. Sure enough, that annoying bird was perched on top of it, squawking away at me once more. These creatures were the primary reason why my walks weren't always peaceful and boring.

"You're the one who should have died!" it cried.

My face twitched slightly as I fought back a grimace. I had to remind myself that I couldn't let it get to me. After all, it'd go away once it got bored. I continued onward, attempting to put the shrieks of my winged stalker out of my mind and hoping it would buzz off sometime soon.

#

When I got to campus, I was only a few minutes late for class and managed to quietly get a seat in the back before the attendance sheet was finished being passed around. Intro to Psych was held in a large lecture hall, and my professor droned on about Sigmund Freud in one of the most dull and flat monotones imaginable. The professor was probably in his sixties, and he carried on with the energy of a funeral march as he read off his slideshow presentation almost word for word. I fidgeted with a pencil in my right hand, unable to muster any motivation to pay attention, let alone take notes. I couldn't help but wonder how people like my professor could hear the sound of their own voice and not get bored listening to themselves. Giving up on the lecture entirely, I started to doodle in my notebook, drawing the backs of the heads of the people who sat in front of me. I didn't have a particular strong love for drawing. It was a hobby I picked up out of boredom more than anything. It was something that occupied my hands when I had nothing else better to do.

"It's your fault!"

The crow thing was now squawking on the professor's podium. My professor carried on with his lecture, blissfully unaware of the foul-looking creature next to him. It wasn't a surprise. As far as I knew, I was the only one who could see something like that damn crow squawking away. It had always been this way. Since I was a little kid, I saw weird monsters that no one else did. I was a child with an overactive imagination and a total pain in the ass to deal with because of it. Nowadays, I carry on as if I don't see them. I tell myself that they are just figments of my imagination, even if they feel like they're more than that sometimes. It was easier this way. As long as I pretended these phantoms didn't exist, I could live a happy, normal life. That's what I'd tell myself at least. Still, the damn bird thing was getting pretty annoying.

This odd creature had been hanging around me for a few months now.

It wouldn't go away, no matter how much I tried to ignore it. The way it shrieked and yelled almost reminded me of my Aunt, Uncle, and Grandma. They were always god-awful company. It didn't matter, though. I was doing just fine now. This was just my normal. As far as I was concerned, that annoying bird could drone on all it liked. I wouldn't let it get to me.

"You're the one who should have died!" it screamed once more.

Please. Flock off already, birdbrain. I quipped to the bird in my head.

Why did it have to be so loud? It was already hard enough to pay attention without a creepy imaginary bird monster screeching the way it was.

"That covers today's material," my professor said. "Please read chapters five and six from the textbook before meeting next Tuesday. Class is dismissed."

I put my notebook and pencil back into my bag and got up, ready to walk out.

"Why won't you pay attention to me, Yuri?" The bird sneered.

I jumped slightly. I couldn't explain what, but something about the phantom suddenly changed in a way that I had never felt before. It gave off an aura of dread that went beyond being a simple and creepy nuisance. It now felt like a predator that caught sight of helpless prey.

"It's your fault, and you know it!" it screamed.

Stop it. You don't know what you're talking about. I replied in my head.

"Better just do everyone a service and die now, you little freak!"

I walked away without looking at the demonic bird, trying not to break into a full run as panic started to set in.

The voices followed me into the hallway, echoing like an orchestra.

"Useless child!"

"Insolent boy!"

"It's your fault!"

I was running now. That thing wasn't real. It was spouting crap. If I kept ignoring it, it would go away. I repeated that train of thought in my head like a chant to reassure myself. I burst out of the main entrance doors, trying to bob and weave through other people as best I could.

"What's wrong, Yuri? I thought I was just a birdbrain who needed to flock off," the bird cried.

I looked up, and the demonic entity was staring down at me while perched on a street lamp. It looked down upon me like a sadistic executioner.

CHAPTER 2

A FATEFUL ENCOUNTER

When I was ten years old, my mom took me to see a doctor.

"He's been panicking about seeing monsters everywhere he goes since his father died. I was hoping it would get better as we set that accident behind us, but…" she trailed off.

The doctor sat across from me.

"These monsters, they aren't real," he said, his voice quiet and gentle. "This is just your brain trying to process some very difficult feelings. Tell me, do you see any monsters in the room with us right now?"

I looked at my mom, who had a creepy-looking canary perched on her shoulder, before looking down at the floor.

"No," I said. "I made it all up. I'm sorry. I shouldn't have lied."

#

I lived the rest of my life ignoring these scary things. The otherworldly, otherwise unseen monsters that clung to people that were only supposed to be figments of my imagination. They've always been there. I've always seen them following other people around, floating around in places like hospitals or graveyards, and even clinging to my mom. They almost always went away if I pretended they weren't there. That's what I told myself over and over again, no matter how hard I had to convince myself. Regardless, as I looked at the eerie, malformed crow, staring down at me like it was ready to kill, I told myself that thing wasn't real. There was no way it could be real.

"Why won't they understand!" the bird screeched. "Why can't they see them?"

I wanted to shout at the bird, to tell it that it had no idea what it was talking about. That I was full of crap.

"I want them to understand!" the crow screeched.

The bird started twitching erratically. I could hear what sounded like bones cracking and snapping as it contorted itself. The crunching sound that invited itself into my ears was sickening. It made me shudder like I'd been splashed with cold water.

"It's my fault!" it roared, its voice tumbling from a high-pitched squeal to a commanding boom. "That's how you feel! Isn't it?"

It felt like a vice was squeezing my skull. My vision blurred as the atmosphere thickened to the point where it felt heavy in my lungs. When I finally came to my senses, it was like time itself had come to a grinding halt. The air was heavy and stagnant. There were no other people as far as the eye could see. All that remained on this campus was this obscene bird-like thing and me.

"You were such a burden..." the bird screeched mockingly.

It made even more foul-sounding crunches as it contorted itself even more violently, slowly mutating and mutilating itself with every crack and pop. It was growing in size, sprouting more wings and eyes. It no longer resembled a bird so much as it did a mass made entirely of jagged wings, bright red eyes, and exposed bones, complete with a stench like that of rotting meat.

"You're better off dead," it roared.

I couldn't move. I was paralyzed by an overwhelming sense of dread that radiated from the beast before me. I couldn't even scream.

"It's time for you to die, Yuri," the monster said. "Sleep eternally."

This was it. I deserved this. It was a fitting end for me. At least my pain would soon be over. The beast spread its wings and swooped down towards me like a bird of prey.

I hoped whatever came next would be quick.

"Die!" it roared.

"Honestly…" a man's voice called, "Do you wish that badly to die? At least *try* to find some reason to keep living!"

Like he suddenly popped into existence, a man appeared before me. He reached out his hand, stopping the monster in its tracks.

"Foul Specter that blights this world," he said with a bright light radiating from his hand,   "I cleanse you of your despair! Begone from this reality!"

A warm light burst from the monster. The overwhelming sense of dread that filled the air faded, slowly replaced with a gentle warmth. The monster gave one last shriek as it burst into a bright flash of light. When it disappeared, I was standing back on campus. The sound of people chattering as they passed once again filled the air. It was like my near-death experience was simply a vivid daydream and nothing more.

The man who banished the beast still stood before me. He was tall, slender, and lanky, with messy red hair. He turned around to face me, his eyes shining like pale blue moons behind his shaggy bangs as he looked me up and down. There was no way he could have been older than thirty, yet he had an air that made him feel wise and world-weary beyond his years. Something about the man's presence felt entirely otherworldly. He gave me an amused smirk.

"Come with me," he said.

Without even getting a moment to attempt to protest, he grabbed me by my arm and dragged me to a nearby bench out of sight from people passing by, practically sitting me down with a small push. I was baffled. Who was this man? Why did he save me?

"Tell me," he said while crossing his arms, "how long have you been able to see them?"

I looked away. I didn't want to answer him. I was shaken to my core, cursing fate yet again. Why did I have to see these awful things? Was this some kind of curse or punishment?   Why did it have to be me?

"Kids these days," the man muttered, exasperated and shrugging his shoulders. "If you don't want to talk to me, that's fine. I'll just give you a piece of advice before I get out of your hair."

The man leaned in and looked square in my eyes, his gaze staunch and direct like an arrow shot from a bow.

"That monster that attacked you is called a 'Specter,'" he said. "That particular type is classified as a Poltergeist. Poltergeists are attracted to repressed emotions. There is something deep inside your heart that you're refusing to accept. If you don't face it, that beast will come back to finish the job, and I won't be there to save you when it does. If you truly want to be free from Specters, you need to accept things as they are."

The man nonchalantly turned around with a fluid turn of his heel.

"With that, I'm off," he said, walking away.

I couldn't stop myself from clenching my jaw at the man's words. They felt forceful and dug deep, and yet they didn't sting. I don't know why, but against my better judgment, I called back to him.

"As long as I can remember," I said.

The man returned his attention to me, almost looking slightly surprised at the sound of my voice.

"I've been able to see those things for as long as I can remember," I said again.

The man returned and sat next to me on the bench.

"Nobody believed me. They said I was making it all up. My mom even took me to a doctor at one point because she was worried I was losing it. I just ended up choking it down all these years, acting like those monsters were never there. I told myself they weren't real over and over again."

I continued to stare down at my feet like a helpless child, my eyes tearing up slightly. I couldn't stop the flow of emotions pouring out of my mouth.

"Even now, I'm terrified that you'll just brush me off like everyone else did!" I stammered. "I'm scared I'll be faking 'normal' for the rest of my life! It terrifies me, and I don't know what to do about it!"

A silence hung in the air as I breathed slowly in and out from the weight of my trauma-laced tirade. This man was going to tell me that I was full of it, just like everyone else; I was sure of it. I was an idiot for unloading like that.

"I believe you," the man replied.

I felt myself go utterly speechless at the man's response. The words "I believe you" felt so alien to me. The man gave a gentle smile.

"I've seen them for a long time, too," he said. "I've made it my life's work to exorcise Specters and preserve this world's balance."

"Exorcise them?" I said. "You mean you can get rid of them?"

The man nodded, his crooked grin both cocky and adventurous.

"My name is Bennet Grey, and I am a mage specializing in exorcising Specters and studying the Malevolence Phenomenon," he said.

Bennet stood up from the bench, turning back to address me, standing bright and tall like a call to adventure personified.

"Would you like to learn how to exorcise them?" he asked.

I felt my chest tighten. Was such a thing even possible? It all felt too good to be true. Despite the doubts I harbored in my brain, I could only give one short and simple answer in response.

"Yes," I replied.

CHAPTER 3

THE MYSTERIOUS MAGE,

BENNET GREY

I didn't have any friends growing up. My dad died in an accident, and while he was smart enough to set up life insurance before he passed away, my mom still worked a lot of hours to keep a steady income going. As a result, I spent most of my childhood at home. Alone. No one wanted anything to do with me. It was only to be expected. I saw monsters that no one else could see, and I was dismissed as a nervous kid with an overactive imagination because of it. I was just another traumatized child. Everyone but my mom thought it was better to avoid me altogether, to avoid being saddled with the trouble.

I spent countless hours reading books to pass the time. My favorite stories were those where a call to adventure would whisk away the protagonist into a crazy world of the unknown. Flash-forward to my life at age twenty, where I had come face-to-face with a strange man calling himself a mage who offered to teach me how to banish the monsters that had plagued my vision for my entire life. It felt like something straight out of a work of fiction.

"I'm sorry," Bennet said with a coy smile, "I didn't quite hear you."

"Yes," I replied, "Teach me to get rid of those things. I don't want to be afraid of them anymore."

Bennet once again smirked, almost like he was pleasantly surprised and intrigued by my answer.

"Come on," he said, "Let's go somewhere better to chat."

Bennet beckoned me with his hand to follow him. We walked around campus for a few minutes, seemingly aimlessly, without a word, until Bennet finally led me into the Student Center.

"Are you looking for something?" I asked while following behind.

"A door," Bennet said.

"Any particular door?" I asked.

"Not really. Just one without any windows."

"Why would we—"

"Here we go! This one will do nicely," Bennet said while stopping in front of a janitor's closet.

"There are better places to talk, you know," I said, sulking in exasperation.

Bennet did not respond. He stroked his index and middle fingers down the center of the door before knocking twice with the back of his knuckle.

"I journey to the Otherside," he said.

Bennet turned the handle and opened the door. On the other side was a large foyer decorated with ornate tapestries. It was a genuine wonder that my jaw didn't hit the floor at the sight.

"Come inside," he said.

"Where's the janitor's closet?" I stammered in stunned confusion.

"Be sure to close the door behind you," Bennet called while walking away.

It was like Bennet was off in his own little world. Would it have killed him to be a little more forthcoming? Throwing caution to the wind, I entered the door, closing it behind me. I emerged into what looked like the front room of an old house. The tapestries that were mounted on the walls depicted things like angels and fairies, and were hung precisely with a great deal of care. The scent of incense and an odor of tobacco wafted throughout the abode, the tobacco smell bordering on pungent. Through the intricately framed windows, I could see cherry blossom petals fall like snow against a bright blue sky that looked like it was painted in a pale blue watercolor.

"You coming?" Bennet's voice called from down the hall.

I hurried to catch up, emerging into a lavender-colored sitting room with potted plants and books scattered all around. Doors at the far end exited onto an open terrace overlooking a wide-open field where more cherry blossom petals fluttered endlessly. In the middle of the room were two deep purple leather couches, facing each other across a coffee table. Bennet was already on the couch farthest from me.

"Sit," he said, gesturing with his hand to the other couch.

I sat down, still somewhat apprehensive of this unusual man who'd invited me to God-knows-where. Saying the situation felt beyond weird would have been an understatement. I'd learned that the things I thought were figments of my imagination were apparently very real monsters called Specters. I was almost killed by a Specter, supposedly known as a Poltergeist. I was saved by a strange man claiming to be an expert on these monsters. Then I followed that same man through a janitor's closet and into a house that felt like it was in another world entirely. The words "baffled confusion" barely scratched the surface of my current feelings. And that was just assuming Bennet was telling the truth, and this wasn't some elaborate scam.

"What is this place?" I asked.

"This is a house built on the Otherside. This area is maintained by a Genius Loci wielding old magic. I've set up shop in this domain to take requests involving exorcising Specters and studying the Malevolence Phenomena," Bennet said. "I also live here."

The Otherside? Malevolence Phenomena? I wasn't sure what to make of the cryptic terms Bennet rattled off.

"I'm sure you are overwhelmed with questions, but for now, let's simply focus on those connected to Specters," Bennet said. "For the time being, at least."

Bennet took a cigarette out of his pocket, then snapped his fingers, causing a small purple flame to appear from his thumb. He used the flame to light the cigarette in his other hand before blowing it out. He pressed the cigarette to his lips, sucking in the nicotine and exhaling a puff of smoke before he spoke once more.

"The Malevolence Phenomenon refers to the cosmic energy that is created by human despair," he said.

"Regret. Sorrow. Anger. Wishes unfilled. All these things and many more create Malevolence. Because of the presence of Malevolence, foul beasts known as Specters are born into this world to haunt and torment the living."

"So, Specters are just monsters made of human despair?" I asked.

Bennet shook his head. "Believe it or not, the supernatural creatures humans call monsters are very different things," he said. "Fae, angels, demons, and what have you are all real beings that live alongside us. Specters are more like abnormalities that tear apart reality itself."

"I don't get it," I said.

"To refer to them collectively, what humans know as 'monsters' are known as 'Others' in my line of work. The beings known as Specters are something different entirely."

"Can you explain it in plain English, so I can understand?" I said, growing more annoyed.

Bennet chuckled. "You're straightforward," he said. "I like that."

He paused, taking another puff from his cigarette.

"How to put this…" he said, grappling for the right words. "Others are living things like you and me, with souls of their very own. They live and die just as we do; granted, they usually live much, much longer. Specters were never alive to begin with."

"What do you mean they're not alive?" I asked.

"Specters don't have souls. They cannot exist without human despair to feed on. They have no desire or ability to think. While some Specters can play the part of an intelligent being, the truth of the matter is that they run on instinct. They only know how to create, stoke, and feed on human despair. They torment the living to sustain themselves, and their mere presence is corrosive to the very fabric of reality here on the Otherside."

I was skeptical. Bennet's explanations all sounded so far-fetched, like something out of a low-budget fantasy anime. His explanations all defied basic human logic.

"This sounds made up," I said.

Bennet's eyes narrowed, his expression both amused and mischievous.

"To any onlooker, a boy who can see monsters that no one else can sounds like something straight out of a work of fiction," he said. "Often, the only people who can see Specters and Others are mages from particular bloodlines—bloodlines that are, to put it bluntly, rapidly dwindling to the point of nonexistence. Yet here you are, with no trace of any such bloodline and in defiance of that truth. You're like a freak of nature."

"Do you have to call me a freak of nature?" I grumbled while scowling at Bennet.

"Sorry," he said while stifling another small laugh. "Believe me when I say I meant it as a compliment. It's not every day I meet someone as fascinating as you are."

Something about the situation still rubbed me the wrong way. I couldn't shake this feeling that Bennet had a deeper motivation beyond his vague curiosity. What was his endgame?

"How do I know you're not lying?" I asked. "That this isn't some scam or something you cooked up."

Bennet scoffed. "After everything you've seen, you still doubt me?" he said with an exaggerated pout.

Bennet sighed before getting up and putting out his cigarette in an ashtray on the coffee table in front of me. He went to rummage through a nearby cabinet and came back with a black candle and a pack of matches. He set the candle on the coffee table and handed the matches to me.

"Perhaps a little divination is in order," he said,

sitting back down. "Do you believe in fate? Or destiny?"

"Nope," I replied flatly.

"To each their own, I suppose," Bennet said while shrugging his shoulders. "Please light the candle for me."

I wasn't sure what this was supposed to prove, but I didn't think it would hurt to play along for the time being. I struck a match against the matchbox, setting it ablaze. I carefully lit the candle, being careful not to burn the tips of my fingers, before blowing out the match. The flame burned for a second, and then it fizzled out instantly. Red smoke wafted up from the candle, wax dripping ever so slightly from the heat of the wick. I stared in confusion as the smoke enveloped and danced around the room, darkening it with a red haze. Bennet started to sway slightly, like he was in a trance. When he spoke, his voice boomed almost like an ethereal echo.

"Yuri Weissman…" he said. "You have lived a difficult life. As a child, you lost your father to a natural disaster that resulted in a flash flood. You were left on the brink of death, having almost drowned in these same waters as your father. Were it not for a first responder who spotted you and resuscitated you when they did, you surely would have perished right then and there."

I was dumbfounded. I hadn't even told Bennet my name, let alone anyone I'd met in the past two years, or what had happened to my dad.

"Since that day, you've lived with what you consider a terrible curse," he said. "You gained the ability to see Specters. You've lived a lonely life as a result of this terrible burden thrust upon you so young, with misfortune only further compounded by the untimely death of your mother four years ago. For a time, you lived among various relatives who blamed you for your mother's death. You've always craved a normalcy that, deep down in your heart, you have always felt you didn't deserve. When the first opportunity presented itself, you set out to live on your own, supported by the money you inherited from your parents when you turned eighteen years old and a generous academic scholarship you had managed to earn with very little effort on your part."

Doubt had been banished from my mind at this point. Bennet was reciting aspects of my past and intimate details that I hadn't spoken about to anyone. Whoever Bennet was, his powers and claims had to be the real deal. This was too elaborate, too otherworldly to be some common scam.

"Now, you fear for your future, unsure of the next step to take in your life. This year will mark a major turning point in your journey," he said.

I stared breathlessly at Bennet, utterly mesmerized by his divination, hanging on every word like I was listening to a passionate storyteller.

"Yuri Weissman," Bennet's voice echoed. "Should you fail to confront the source of the sorrow that haunts your past this coming year, your soul will never know peace. Only a life of misery will await you."

The smoke started to fade, and I was left overwhelmed with the heavy weight of all that I had learned and was now forced to accept. There was no turning back…

CHAPTER 4

IN DEFIANCE OF DESPAIR

The silence was deafening. How do you respond to the revelation that everything you believed to be real for most of your life was wrong? How do you react when you are told your very future is potentially set for a vague, impending doom? These were questions I frantically tried to grapple with as I sat across from Bennet, emotionally paralyzed by the truckload of information that had been dumped on me.

"What do you intend to do next, Yuri?" Bennet asked.

I sat quietly, not even sure how to verbalize my confusion.

"It's only natural you'd be left feeling confused and afraid after experiencing and learning the things you have today," Bennet said, "But do you remember what you said before you came here? About why you wanted to come?"

"That I didn't want to be afraid of Specters anymore," I said.

"I assume your answer hasn't changed."

"No," I replied meekly.

Bennet gave me a satisfied smile. "Then hold onto that resolve," he said. "Use it to guide your way, even when the path ahead seems uncertain."

I looked down at the floor. It was a lot to take in all at once. I wondered if this is what it meant to "accept things as they are." It was easier said than done. Still, the only way I could keep moving forward was to acknowledge this ugly truth laid out in front of me.

"Okay," I said.

Bennet got up, putting away the candle and matches he had gotten out earlier. He came back with a jagged piece of stone that resembled jade or malachite, with straps of leather bound around it, like it was meant to be worn as some sort of pendant.

"Take this," he said while handing me the stone by the leather string.

"What is it?" I asked.

"It's a gem made of crystalized magic," he said, "As long as you have it on you, I can communicate with you from a great distance. It will also help ward off weaker Specters. Think of it as being like a good luck charm."

I took the gem from Bennet and placed it in my pocket.

"With that," he said, "You are officially my apprentice. I look forward to working with you."

"I'll try my best..." I replied, unable to replicate Bennet's enthusiasm.

#

Bennet led me back to the foyer of his house.

"Head through that door, and you'll be back at that janitor's closet we entered through," he said. "Take some time to reflect on everything you learned today. I'll reach out to you tomorrow so we can go over the finer details of your training."

"Alright," I replied.

"Rest well until then," he said in a playful tone.

I exited the strange pocket world, apparently called the Otherside, and returned to the student center. I emerged from the janitor's closet, making sure to close it behind me.

I wasn't sure what to think or feel now. Specters, Others, and Bennet Grey. Each felt like a baffling mystery I could barely wrap my head around. The only thing I knew for sure was that they were all real things and not simply figments of my imagination. They existed, whether I liked it or not. There was no denying it anymore. It was even more frightening, in a way. These things weren't simply some trick of the eye that I could ignore while I went about my day. What was my next step supposed to be? Accept things as they are? How? Everything felt like one giant pill that was suffocating to swallow.

I finally came to my senses after having gotten lost in my thoughts for so long. The student center was almost empty now. It was late. It seemed like my next step would be to go home and hope I'd wake up in a normal world the next morning, realizing this had all been a dream.

When I stepped outside, the sun was starting to set, and the streetlights were flickering to life. I looked at the sky, which was now orange, like marmalade. I hated sunsets. They always brought me back to that day. I could only see sunsets as ugly things that served as a painful reminder of what I'd lost.

Reigning in my disgust, I readjusted the straps of my bag on my shoulders, placed my hands in the pockets of my windbreaker, and walked back to my apartment.

#

Despite my confusion, that night played out as any other. I heated a frozen lasagna in the microwave for dinner, took a shower, and then finished reading the sci-fi novel I'd started the day before. I eventually fell asleep.

When I woke up the following morning, the previous day felt like it had been a hazy dream. I would have breathed a massive sigh of relief if it were. Unfortunately, sitting on a folding table I was using as a makeshift nightstand was the green charm Bennet gave me—a cruel reminder of the reality of the world I lived in.

It was a Saturday, meaning I didn't have any classes.

I loafed around my apartment, unable to focus on schoolwork, bored and restless. Waiting to hear back from Bennet had me sitting on pins and needles. Eventually, the day turned into evening, and when I was just about to give up on hearing back from him entirely, the charm next to my bed started to glow.

"Good evening," a voice echoed coming from the bright green stone.

I quickly grabbed the pendant by the string, holding it so that the stone was level with my face.

"Is that you, Bennet?" I asked.

"I told you I would be contacting you through this charm, didn't I?" he replied. "I assume you're ready to begin your training?"

"Of course I am," I replied with a grumble, "That's what we agreed to do. I was hoping you would have called me sooner."

"That excited to hear from little old me?" Bennet said.

I could already picture Bennet's annoying, coy smile from the other side of the line.

Why does he have to be like this… I thought to myself in annoyance.

"So, what now?" I asked.

"I want you to find a closed door with no windows. Make sure to bring that charm with you," Bennet said.

I placed the pendant in my front pocket before proceeding to my apartment's front door.

"Okay," I said.

"You remember how we entered my shop yesterday, yes?" Bennet asked.

"How could I forget?" I replied. "It's not every day some rando takes you through a janitor's closet and into another world."

"Fair point," Bennet mused. "I'm going to teach you the charm I used back then. This spell links a doorway to another one in the Otherside. As long as you're using a door you can't see through and you have a clear idea of where you want to go, you can use this spell to travel to the Otherside anytime you like."

I felt my shoulders and stomach tense up at the prospect of this task.

"Right now?" I asked. "Is something like that even possible for me?"

"You won't know unless you try," he said, almost mockingly.

I clapped my hands to my cheeks, trying to settle my nerves.

"What do I do?" I asked.

"For this spell," Bennet said, "I need you to picture my home on the Otherside in your mind's eye. Can you do that?"

"Yes," I replied.

"Good," Bennet said. "After you've pictured the location in your mind, you need to take two of your fingers and stroke them down the center of the door. Finally, knock on the door twice with the back of your knuckle and say
'I journey to the Otherside.'"

I stood in front of my apartment door, mentally preparing myself for what was to come.

"Don't lose your focus. You must keep your destination in your mind until the door is opened," Bennet said.

I took two deep breaths, clearing my mind as I tried to conjure the image of Bennet's home in my mind. I recalled the vivid tapestries that adorned the foyer I entered. I recalled the dark purple couches and the various potted plants and books that littered Bennet's sitting room.

I recalled the cherry blossom petals that fluttered outside the windows like snow. I recalled the faint smell of incense and the stench of tobacco that I smelled when I first entered. Finally, I recalled the profound impact I felt when Bennet divined my fortune. I took another deep breath, hyper-fixating on these details the best I could. With my eyes still closed, I stroked my index and middle fingers down the center of my door and knocked twice with the back of my knuckles.

"I journey to the Otherside," I said.

With my eyes still shut, I opened the door. I nervously clenched my jaw as I slowly opened my eyes. To my amazement, right outside my front door was the entryway to Bennet's house in the Otherside. I stepped through the entryway while closing the door behind me, still in disbelief at what I had accomplished.

"You did well," Bennet called from down the hall.

I followed the sound of his voice back to the same sitting room from yesterday, where Bennet was reclining on the farthest couch, smoking a cigarette once more. On the coffee table in front of him sat what looked like an antique birdcage made of black cast iron.

"Sit," he said.

I sat down across from him like I did the first time I came here. "Is that a spell anyone can use?" I asked.

Bennet took a puff from his cigarette before exhaling a small amount of smoke. "Ordinary people usually cannot travel to and from the Otherside freely," he said. "But you and I are *not* ordinary people."

Bennet had called this place the Otherside several times already, but I still didn't quite understand what it meant.

"What exactly is 'The Otherside?'" I asked.

"I trust you recall the beings I mentioned yesterday, yes?" he asked.

"Others, you mean?"

"Good. This should make this conversation easier, then."

Bennet put out his cigarette in the nearby ashtray before sitting up straight, staring directly into my eyes. "If I told you the world you know was only a third of a bigger whole…would you believe me?" he asked.

"Come again?" I replied, not understanding his question

"The world as you know it is essentially one of three distinct parts," Bennet said. "The Nearside, where humans reside, and the rules of reality are at their most absolute. The Otherside, where the beings humans consider supernatural entities are born, and reality is flimsy and flexible. Finally, the Farside, where the souls of the departed journey after death. It's the place where all human magic is born."

"I don't think I one hundred percent understand, but after everything else I've seen and heard, it doesn't surprise me," I said with slight exasperation, almost unfazed.

Between the beings called Others, the things called Specters, and the walking, talking, cigarette-smoking enigma sitting in front of me, I didn't think anything else regarding the nature of the world's very existence could've rattled me anymore.

"So we're here on the Otherside now?" I asked.

"That's correct," Bennet said. "As long as you have a clear destination in mind, you can use that spell to travel from the Nearside to anywhere in the Otherside you feel like."

"Like my apartment, or anywhere at school?" I said.

"Yes," Bennet replied before leaning towards me, his eyes cold and serious. "A word of advice, though. Don't lose sight of your destination when you use that spell. It can end pretty badly. Should you fail to properly picture your destination when casting this magic, stepping through the door could drop you anywhere in the Otherside. It's not exactly a place you just want to wander around. Trust me."

I grimaced at the thought of what could have happened had I screwed up earlier. My discomfort must have been painfully obvious, because Bennet continued.

"The reason I asked you to bring that charm with you is so that if you were to accidentally wander off into this strange world, I can track you down. Also, keep in mind that if you're ever really stuck in a bind, returning through the door you entered will take you back to where you came from," Bennet said.

"Okay..." I replied, almost disturbed by how casual he was about all of this

At that moment, my eyes drifted to the cage on the coffee table in front of me. I stared in horror as I saw what resided inside. Behind the black iron bars was a grayed and shriveled severed hand with dark black claws, just lying in the cage, limp and completely still. It gave off a familiar stench of rotting meat that had been partially obscured by the smell of Bennet's earlier cigarette.

"What is that?" I asked, fearing I already knew the answer.

"It's a Specter," Bennet replied. "A Ghoul, to be more precise. They're small fry who haven't managed to find a victim to cling to or haunt yet. Usually, when a Ghoul finds a host, it adapts itself into a form in which it can most optimally stoke and feed on suffering. That's where we get the more powerful classifications of Specters, like the Poltergeist haunting you yesterday."

"Why is it here?" I asked, my stomach churning slightly at the sight of it.

"Would you relax? I made sure to render it into a comatose state before I brought it here," Bennet said. "Besides, how are you supposed to learn how to banish Specters if you don't have one to practice on? No time like the present to start learning the fundamentals!"

I gaped uncomfortably at the shriveled Ghoul hand. Just looking at it made me uncomfortable. Why did it have to smell like rotting meat?

"Is right now the *best* time?" I asked. "These things are so weird and gross…"

Bennet tilted his head, brandishing a smug smirk. "I'm sorry, would you prefer to practice the basics against a berserk monster fighting to kill?" he said with a playful bite to his voice.

I fought back an annoyed glare in response to the scathing accuracy of Bennet's sarcasm. "Point taken…" I muttered back. "So, what do I do?"

Bennet extended his hand over the cage. "Hold your hand out like this and imagine or recall something that gives you strength. The best way to fight despair incarnate is hope, after all."

"What do you mean by hope?" I asked.

"Like I said. Specters are despair incarnate. The only way to combat them is to purge them of that despair," Bennet explained. "Darkness and despair, light and hope. They are two sides of the same coin. To overcome and cleanse a Specter, you need to channel that light. The resolve to never give up. The desire to protect others. Happy memories of past days. Use those emotions and thoughts to stand against the

Specters before you. Unlike other magic, the spells we use to exorcise Specters are given power by those feelings. Without a proper resolve, the motions and incantations would be useless."

I looked down at the shriveled hand once again. I didn't understand how positive thinking or whatever was supposed to get rid of Specters. However, Bennet had said it was the best way to exorcise them, and I didn't have any other ideas on how to get rid of them.

I reluctantly held my hand over the cage. I closed my eyes, searching my brain for something, anything positive that might have fit the bill for what Bennet was talking about. All I knew was that I didn't want to deal with Specters, and I didn't wanna be burdened with my emotional baggage all the time.

The avoidance of pain, I thought to myself. *That's what I'll channel. I think that will work—*

"Stop," Bennet said coldly.

I jumped at the sudden sound of the mage's voice. His eyes were serious, and his voice firm.

"Your thoughts were along the lines of 'I don't want to get hurt anymore,' weren't they?" Bennet said.

"Yes," I replied with a blank stare.

Bennet shook his head, looking slightly disappointed.

"That won't work," he said. "Sadness, anger, and pain… those things are unavoidable parts of the human experience. To shy away from all suffering entirely would be like trying to avoid living altogether. It's a crappy way to spend one's life, and poorly suited for exorcising Specters. Had I let you continue, you would have given that Ghoul a hearty meal to chew on, and it would have become violent," Bennet said.

I looked down at the ground, Bennet's disappointment weighing on my consciousness like an iron ball and chain.

"I'm sorry," I said.

"Don't be," Bennet replied.

I looked back up at Bennet. His expression was relaxed as his stern scowl shifted to that of a reassuring grin.

"You literally just began learning, so it would be unfair to expect you to get it right away," he said, "I assume you're willing to keep trying?"

"Yeah," I replied while regaining my composure.

"Then chin up," Bennet said. "To exorcise a Specter is to defy despair itself. The moment you give up is the moment you've lost."

I still couldn't get a read on Bennet. He was annoying and needlessly cryptic. It wouldn't have surprised me if he liked messing with people just for the fun of it. Despite that, he'd saved my life earlier, offered me the chance to learn more about the Specters I'd been afraid of all my life, and reassured me when I got down on myself. I had no idea what was going on in his head, but he was my best bet for figuring out what to do about these creepy Specters that I saw everywhere. For the being, I would put my faith in him.

Bennet stretched his arms before reclining on the couch like a cat about to take a nap. "I'm getting hungry, so let's take a break," he said. "Why don't you do your wise teacher a solid and pick him up something to eat? It's pretty trashy, but instant ramen sounds great right now."

"Since when did I become your errand boy?" I replied, practically groaning.

"I mean, I'm only teaching you lifesaving skills here," Bennet said playfully. "Part of our arrangement was that you'd act as an assistant in my work."

I suddenly got a better understanding of Bennet's endgame. As much as it annoyed me, Bennet wasn't wrong in that he was teaching me something that could ultimately save my life one day.

"Fine…" I grumbled.

I stood up and departed from the sitting room.

"Don't be afraid to pick something up for yourself as well," Bennet called as I left.

What I didn't realize as I left the Otherside and returned to my apartment was that the errand I was about to run would soon herald my first "client" working alongside the mysterious mage, Bennet Grey.

CHAPTER 5

THE GIRL HAUNTED

BY A POLTERGEIST

It was a short five-minute walk from my apartment to the nearest convenience store. The sun had already set, and the waxy yellow glow of streetlights and the light of the moon up above were the only things that cut through the darkness. The night air was cold against my skin, but in a way that almost felt refreshing after the craziness I'd had to deal with in the last twenty-four hours. When I got to the door of the convenience store, I saw a bright green flyer plastered on a nearby window. It read:

The Grimoire: News of the Occult, Aliens, and All Things Weird.

The flier was decorated with weird-looking symbols and smaller pictures of UFOs, aliens, and pentagrams. I couldn't help but scowl in annoyance in response. I spent my entire life living an experience that came straight out of a ghost story.

Why the hell do people enjoy these things so much? Don't they have anything else better to do with their time? I thought to myself while glaring at the green piece of paper.

Attempting to let go of my irritation, I pulled open the door and went inside. The store was quiet, and I was fortunate enough to find instant ramen down the first aisle I went down. I grabbed the cheapest package I could find, since Bennet never told me what flavor he wanted, and brought it up to the cashier.

A girl was already checking out when I got in line. She was petite, wearing a black shirt and fashionably torn skinny jeans, carrying a red plaid purse. Her dark hair was cut in a short, jagged bob, with a bright pink streak dyed around her bangs. The cashier scanned the single energy drink she brought to the register.

"That'll be two dollars and seventy-five cents," the cashier said.

As the girl went to rummage through her purse, I heard a weird snickering from behind me. I turned around to see what looked like a creepy, vaguely rabbit-like stuffed animal thing peering from behind one of the shelves, holding a black leather wallet in its paws. It was like a demonic toy from a low-budget horror film. It gave off an aura of dread that I was uncomfortably too familiar with.

"I'm sorry," the girl said, "I think I dropped my wallet somewhere. I can't pay for it."

After an awkward exchange, the cashier set the energy drink down on the counter, and the girl went off to look for her wallet. The creepy rabbit Specter snickered once more.

"Did you find everything alright, sir?" the cashier asked as I stepped up to the register.

"Yeah," I replied, only half paying attention.

The girl had given up searching for her wallet and walked outside. The Specter followed after her, tossing the leather wallet it was holding aside as it did.

"That'll be one dollar and five cents," the cashier said.

After I paid for Bennet's instant ramen, I grabbed the wallet the Specter had stolen from the girl it was stalking. I didn't typically like getting involved with other people like this, and it was usually better to mind my own business, but something wasn't right. I was certain that it was a Specter, and unlike a lot of the ones I've seen before, it seemed to be actively harassing that girl. I wanted to make sure she was okay before I did anything else.

#

I emerged outside, looking up and down the sidewalk to see if I could spot the girl from before. When I turned to my right, I saw her walking away about two blocks down.

"Hey!" I called

She continued along, probably unable to hear me. I ran after her, trying to catch up and managing to close the distance some.

"Hey!" I called again. "I think you dropped this!"

As the girl turned around, I heard the Specter's snickering once more. I looked up to see the demonic rabbit standing on top of a window AC unit mounted above her.

"Look out below!" the Specter cackled.

The AC unit started to make a loud creaking sound.

"Watch out!" I shouted

I don't know what happened, but before I even realized what I was doing, I had bolted and tackled the girl out of the way. As I did, the AC unit crashed into the ground behind both of us. The girl and I both landed sprawled on the ground. I was breathing heavily from the adrenaline pumping through my veins.

"I'm sorry," I stammered in between huffs.

The girl stared at both me and the now-destroyed AC unit that had almost crushed her. After a brief pause, she got to her feet and dusted herself off.

"Thanks a million!" she said while reaching out a hand to help me to my feet. "I'd be a pancake right now if it weren't for you."

"Oh, uh…yeah. You're welcome," I replied awkwardly, very unused to being shown gratitude.

I took a moment to scope out the area, making sure the Specter wasn't still hanging around or about to make another homicide attempt. I finally breathed a sigh of relief when I couldn't spot the Specter or hear the sound of its sinister snickering. It was probably safe to assume that it had made itself scarce.

Suddenly, like being struck with a bolt of lightning, I quickly remembered why I had followed the girl to begin with.

"You dropped this back there," I said, handing the girl her wallet.

"Thanks," she said again, slightly surprised.

The girl looked me up and down as though she was trying to recall something.

"Are you a student at Clover?" she asked.

"Yeah," I replied. "How'd you know?"

The girl placed her hand on her hip. "I've seen you around on campus," she said. "I'm a psych major there. My name's Amy. Nice to meet ya!"

"I'm Yuri," I replied.

I paused, finding myself worried, wondering if the Specter stalking Amy had attempted anything like this before.

"Does stuff like this happen to you a lot?" I asked.

"Like you wouldn't believe," Amy said with a weary moan. "Bad luck has just been following me around lately. Somehow, I always lose things as soon as I need them, or stuff like my computer or my phone will randomly go haywire on me, just narrowly avoiding some petty accidents."

Amy then gestured with her hand towards the AC unit that had almost crushed her.

"As you can see, luck hasn't exactly been on my side as of late," she said. "I'm beginning to think I might be cursed or something."

If only she knew… I wryly thought to myself.

It was probably safe to assume that Specter was stalking and tormenting her. I made a mental note to bring it up to Bennet later.

"Oh, that reminds me," Amy said, her eyes lighting up a little. "Speaking of curses, you should check out my magazine."

Amy reached into her bag and pulled out a green flyer. It was the same one I had seen on the convenience store window, advertising that odd "news of the weird" website called The Grimoire. Great. She was an occult fanatic. Just peachy.

"I have to get back to my apartment to finish doing some research for a story I'm working on," Amy said. "Thanks again for earlier. I'll make sure to say hi the next time I see you on campus."

With that, Amy went on her way, an excited spring in her step.

"Well, well," Bennet called. "Aren't you a natural?"

I was startled as he emerged from the shadows behind me.

"How long have you been there?" I asked.

"I got worried when I sensed a Specter near my new hire while he was running an errand for me," Bennet teased. "Naturally, I thought I'd stay close and intervene if needed. You handled the situation beautifully. You didn't need my help at all."

"If you were here the entire time, why didn't you exorcise that Specter?" I said while trying to restrain an exasperated scowl.

Bennet threw his hands up in the air as he shook his head. "Have you already forgotten?" he said, "You remember what I said when I exorcised that Poltergeist that was haunting you, right?"

I scowled, looking away from his annoying face as I begrudgingly conceded his point. "You said that if I didn't come to terms with my feelings, the Specter would come back," I said in a flat, irritated tone, trying not to grind my teeth.

"Bingo," Bennet replied. "Specters are attracted to, and feed on, the darkness in human hearts. That girl has something locked away inside that's too painful for her to confront. That Poltergeist feeds on it and causes misfortune, creating more despair to feed on."

"What happens if she can't shake the Specter?" I asked.

Bennet directed his gaze in the direction Amy had departed. "A great many things can happen," he said. "But the most likely outcome with how that Poltergeist is behaving is that it will kill her before moving on to another victim."

I anxiously scratched at my throat for a moment, trying to ignore the anxious, guilty knot forming in my stomach. "Should we do something about it?" I asked.

"Do you *want* us to do something about it?" Bennet asked.

I thought back to the Poltergeist that tried to kill me. I thought back to my mom and that day four years ago that I had been constantly reliving in my nightmares. The idea of getting myself involved with another sticky situation like that made my skin crawl. But the idea of doing nothing and leaving Amy probably to die felt even worse. I couldn't look at a Specter like some imaginary monster I could ignore anymore. After all that had happened, I don't think I could ever live with myself if Amy died and I knowingly did nothing about it.

"I want to save her from the Specter," I said. "If it's possible, I mean."

Bennet gave me a satisfied smile, looking like he was amused at the prospect of things to come.

"It's indeed possible if you're willing to try to make that outcome reality," Bennet said. "I'll reach out to you first thing in the morning so we can devise a plan of attack together. Here's to hunting our first Specter together, Yuri."

CHAPTER 6

A NEWFOUND RESOLVE

I stood on a rooftop, the sky a creamy orange like the color of marmalade from the setting sun. A gentle breeze blew against my face.

How many times have I stood upon this rooftop now? How many times have I revisited this memory? How many times have I revisited this pain and sorrow? I cannot recall.

I watched in horror as my mom stood on the rooftop's ledge with an eerie, otherworldly canary perched on her shoulder.

"Mom!" I screamed.

My mother turned back to look at me, a weak smile on her face. She then closed her eyes and stepped off the ledge. I fell to my knees as everything went utterly silent. In that moment, my entire world shattered before my eyes. I couldn't even hear the sound of my own screaming.

#

I was groggy when I woke up the next day. The morning sun peeked through my apartment as I mustered the motivation to pull myself out of bed. I'd lost count of how many times I'd had that dream by now. That painful memory is burned deep into my brain.

It doesn't matter; I have things I need to do today, I thought to myself stubbornly.

Bennet had told me he'd reach out today with a plan on how to handle the Specter haunting Amy. I could only wait for the usual glow from Bennet's charm until then.

After I had gotten out of bed, feeling like a zombie rising from the grave, I took a warm shower to try to wake myself up. Once I had dried off and gotten dressed, I made a cup of instant coffee and sat at a small table to eat a toasted English muffin slathered in peanut butter I had made for breakfast. Bored and with nothing better to do, I scrolled through some of the local news headlines on my phone as I waited for my coffee's caffeine to kick in. It was all the usual doom and gloom. A woman's murder that played for ratings and entertainment value, general hearsay and gossip, and finally, a wholesome human-interest story about someone who found their dog that went missing a few months ago.

Bennet's charm and Amy's flyer sat on the table in front of me as I mindlessly scrolled. As my gaze drifted away from internet drama to the flyer on the table, a thought occurred to me. No matter what it was they wrote, writers often revealed much about themselves through their content without even realizing it. I couldn't stand ghost stories or any of that crap, but Amy had enough love to actively research and write about the paranormal. It was possible I could get a better understanding of what kind of person she was if I read what she wrote.

I opened a new tab on my phone's web browser and typed "The Grimoire News of the Weird" into the search bar. Thankfully, it was the first result on the search engine. It was one of those custom blog websites where you could customize your entire layout and URL. "The Grimoire" was written in a lime green bold serif-typeface in the header, with the tagline "Your destination for all things supernatural." Underneath were several posts with their titles written in the same green font, with a preview of their content under them, along with the date they'd been posted. I tapped on the most recent article listed at the top of the page, titled "The Famous Crying Baby Bridge of Clover."

#

On the outskirts of Clover, there's an old wooden plank bridge on the Pine Hills Hiking Trail. The bridge runs over a rushing river, and supposedly, late at night, you can hear the sound of a baby crying underneath. Legend has it that a long time ago, a woman drowned her child in that river. Overcome with guilt for what she had done, she drowned herself in that same body of water. Reported sightings also claim that late at night, you can see the shadow of the woman floating above the waters, desperately searching for the body of her lost child. Records from the local historical society have indicated a handful of deaths in that river, including one of a baby. However, the circumstances beyond that are long forgotten. I ventured out there late one night to confirm the reports. While I was unable to hear the sound of the crying or see the shadow of the woman, I will continue searching until I can fully verify or debunk these claims. I have a few theories

#

The article carried on. The attention to detail Amy put into it was impressive. It felt like a waste that she didn't apply that talent to something more useful. The article had fifty views and one comment. The comment simply read:

You're a crazy bitch!

I looked through more of Amy's posts. Each article involved her meticulously researching some urban legend, then being disappointed when she couldn't find anything when she visited the sites, while still holding out hope of finding some definitive proof of the supernatural in the future. All the while, each post had one or two comments, and every one of them involved someone making fun of her. Some of the comments even outright mentioned Clover College.

Cyberbullying... The scum in the comments section needed better things to do with their lives, I thought to myself, ignoring the bitter taste the sight left in my mouth.

I didn't get it, though. Why would Amy keep hunting down and writing these ghost stories when all anyone did was make fun of her for it? I picked up the flier and held it in my right hand, staring at the bright green letters. Why did Amy care about this so much? Why did it matter to her?

All of a sudden, my vision started to blur. It felt like someone was forcing a metal rod into my forehead.

"Please! Someone! Notice me!" Amy's voice echoed. *"I don't wanna be alone anymore!"*

The pain started to ease as quickly as it came. I sat doubled over, breathing heavily.

"Something troubling you, kiddo?" Bennet's voice called.

As I came to my senses, I noticed the charm once again giving off a green glow.

"It's nothing," I grumbled. "And I'm not a kid."

"Lighten up, will you?" Bennet said. "Somebody's not a morning person…"

I took a deep breath before I spoke next, trying not to let Bennet's antics get the best of me.

"You said you'd have a plan on how to exorcise the Specter haunting Amy," I said.

"I do," Bennet replied.

"What is it?"

I could already picture Bennet brandishing some sort of shit-eating grin as he prepared to relay his plan to me.

"The plan is quite a simple one, actually," he said. "Since you both attend the same college, the best way to learn what caused the Poltergeist to start haunting her is to befriend her."

I grimaced, thinking back to Amy's website and her obsession with the occult.

"Is that the best way?" I groaned.

"Come on now, don't be such a loner!" Bennet teased.

"I'm not a loner!" I snapped back. "I just can't stand people who get so excited about ghost stories and the occult."

"All jokes aside, Yuri, this is the easiest way to help her," Bennet said. "Most people, even 'believers,' won't believe you if you tell them they're being haunted by a manifestation of despair. Even on the off chance that they did believe, alerting them to the presence of the Specter haunting them could cause even more problems. These things are attracted to and feed off the darkness in human hearts after all. If we're not careful, we could easily do more harm than good."

I leaned back in my chair, letting my arms dangle at my sides. Bennet had a point. Most people tended to get defensive when their faults were pointed out to them, especially if it was something they're insecure about deep down. I was already hesitant to believe Bennet's explanations about Specters, and that was after I'd been able to see them for most of my life. We could've ultimately made a Specter stronger if we weren't smart about it. As I stared up at my apartment ceiling, I thought back to the recurring memory that haunted my dreams.

"I know this is off-topic, Bennett," I said, "but when you were teaching me about the Otherside yesterday, you said something about a place called 'The Sea of Souls' and how it houses the departed spirits of humans and Others. That's basically where people go when they die, right? Kind of like Heaven or something?"

"In a sense," Bennet said somberly. "An Other known as the Collector guides the souls of the deceased there, catalogs their names, records their deaths, and then watches over them as they await rebirth."

"So it's basically like reincarnation?" I asked. "The person is gone forever, but the soul carries on? And it happens for everyone?"

"Yes," Bennet replied, "As long as the soul is intact enough to make the journey, it will always have a chance to begin anew."

I bit my lip. "Is that so?" I thought aloud.

I took a deep breath, taking a long exhale before I sat back up in my chair and stared down at Bennet's charm.

"I've never been good at talking with people. I've never had a friend my own age before either," I said. "I'm not sure if I'll be able to 'befriend' Amy, but based on what you said, she'll probably die if we don't do anything, right?"

"That's right," Bennet said. "At the rate she's going, that Specter will probably kill her long before she figures out what's happening. Does the thought of that bother you?"

I could practically feel Bennet probing as he asked the question. Amy was just a stranger to me at the end of the day, and I could easily walk away and do nothing. Even knowing that, though, I couldn't just carry on like I hadn't seen anything. I wasn't just a powerless bystander anymore, and I knew that Specters were real things that could do some real harm when left unchecked. That's why I felt compelled to take action, even if I didn't want to.

"Alright, Bennet," I said begrudgingly. "We'll do it your way."

CHAPTER 7

AN UNEXPECTED WARNING

I used to always sit by myself during lunch when I was in school. I couldn't bring myself to get close to people. I learned how to draw because I got bored and didn't have anything else to do with my time. Once, when I was eleven years old and sitting by myself at lunch like usual, a boy I went to school with finally came to talk to me. I couldn't tell you what his name was, let alone recall what he looked like, but I remembered our conversation vividly.

"Why are you sitting by yourself?" he asked.

"Just cause," I said, not even so much as glancing in his direction as I drew an apple from my lunch in a notebook.

The boy looked down at my sketch.

"Wow! You're really good!" the boy said with genuine surprise.

"I got bored with drawing stick figures," I replied bluntly.

The boy sat down across from me. "Do you have any other drawings I can see?" he asked.

I had finally lifted my face from my notebook and made eye contact with the boy. An eerie, two-headed black snake with blood-red eyes was wrapped around his neck and resting its heads on his right shoulder. I couldn't stand the sight of it. The monster, which I would one day come to learn was called a Specter, terrified me. When I saw the Specter that clung to that boy, I did what I always did. I buried my heart deep down and pushed him away.

I didn't even bother to mince words.

"I'm sorry," I said, "I don't wanna talk to you."

I packed up my things and walked away. The boy probably thought I was a jerk for giving him the cold shoulder like that and hated me for it. I didn't blame him, though. I was used to it. I could see monsters that haunted people that no one else could. Even though I convinced myself that it was merely my overactive imagination, I did everything I could to keep those monsters at a distance, even if it meant pushing away the people they haunted. No one once believed that I could see such horrible things until the day I met Bennet.

I knew deep down that loneliness and isolation would be the only constants in my life. I told myself for a long time that I was okay with it. It was a curse someone had to bear, and I was the unlucky one who drew the short straw. That was life, and there was nothing I could do about it.

#

That Monday was a cloudy and gray one. This would be my first day attending classes after meeting Bennet and coming to terms with the nature of my power. It felt weird trying to carry on like normal, knowing what I knew now. Learning that humanity was plagued by unseeable monsters attracted to human despair or that other realities were living alongside our own wasn't something you just accept and move on from like some proverbial bump in the road. It all felt so heavy.

As I walked to campus, I thought about what Bennet said about befriending Amy being the best way to save her from the Poltergeist haunting her. He wasn't wrong about that; even if Amy was a genuine believer in the supernatural, she wouldn't believe me if I told her about Specters. Hell, I saw the damn things every day, and I convinced myself that it was all in my head until very recently. That being said, I had no idea how I'd "befriend" Amy. I was already socially awkward with people to begin with, and I couldn't stand people who get so into ghost stories and that crap. I saw things that looked like they came right out of the pages of a Lovecraft novel every day, and I would've given anything not to see them anymore. It both baffled and annoyed me that people would actively look for something like these monstrosities.

Thinking about Amy's articles on the Grimoire, she didn't come across as some blind, devoted believer in the occult. She wrote as if she needed to convince herself they were real and worth searching for. She referenced not only urban legends, but also historical records, environmental reports, and the like. When investigations ended in her being unable to confirm a haunting, she never tried to rationalize and justify the dead end as a fluke. She always ended the article by saying something along the lines of how she'd keep searching, even if she hadn't found anything yet.

Then there was when I heard her voice holding the flyer she gave me the other night. I'm not sure what that was about. Was I hearing true feelings or something else? I never experienced anything like that. Then again, I never really tried to understand someone else until now.

I wanted to chalk up what I heard as simply being tired and imagining things, but it felt too real to go along with that line of thought. I'd heard Amy's voice as clear as day, I'm certain of that. There was something about her tone and the pain I felt in my head at the time that made it feel just as real as the Specters or the Otherside. I realized I should probably mention it to Bennet the next time we talk, but I suspected he'd probably give me a bunch of cryptic answers or a stream of magic babble I wouldn't understand. He said he'd watch from a distance using the charm he gave me, and that he would intervene if the Specter happened to go berserk and needed to be subdued. That was better than nothing.

I finally arrived on campus. I didn't have the faintest idea of how I'd even begin searching for Amy. Perhaps it was best to start asking around at the psych building, since Amy said she was a psychology major —

"You," a voice called from behind me.

I jumped as I turned to confront the speaker. Standing before me was a tall man with short, neatly combed hair. He wore a charcoal grey suit, like a businessman's, and half-rim glasses with dark frames. His skin was pale and waxy, his face young, but with sharp features that made his serious expression all the more intimidating.

"You. Are you the human called Yuri Weissman?" he asked, his voice a flat and even monotone.

"What if I am?" I replied.

"I've reason to believe that he has become acquainted with a mage known as Bennet Grey," the man said. "I have something to say to him of the utmost urgency."

I didn't like the feeling I got from this man. He wasn't a Specter, but he sure as shit wasn't human. I could get that much at least. Was he an Other?

"What's the message?" I asked.

The man examined me, his gaze shrewd as he looked me up and down

"If I were to meet Yuri," the man said, the passive aggression in his tone very overt, "I would tell him to sever all ties with Bennet Grey."

My knuckles tightened. "Why would you say that?" I asked.

"The boy known as Yuri Weissman is quite famous in my circle," he said. "Near-death experiences are far from out of the ordinary, but very few humans have made contact with the Sea of Souls on the Farside and still managed to return despite all of that. I worry about someone taking advantage of him."

"Take advantage?" I parroted back.

The man dropped all pretense. "Bennet Grey is an affront to the natural order," he said coldly. "He is a ticking time bomb of misfortune that will bring everything around him to ruin. It is in your best interest to sever all ties with him, Yuri Weissman."

Before I could respond, I heard Amy's voice. "Hey, Yuri!" she called.

I turned and saw that Amy had just emerged from a classroom building and was walking towards me. When I spun back toward the foreboding man who had just given me a dire warning, I found he had vanished without a trace, like he was never there to begin with. Too many questions spiraled in my head at once, and I had too little time to sort them out. As Amy approached me, I only had mere moments to change gears entirely.

"Were you talking to someone just now?" Amy asked.

"I was just thinking out loud about some stuff I could draw," I lied.

"Oh, cool. Are you any good?" Amy said.

"It's a casual hobby, but I'm not terrible," I replied, carefully putting on a rehearsed, friendly smile with calculated ease.

"I can't even draw a stick figure, so you're probably way better than I am," Amy said. "I've been thinking about commissioning some illustrations for my articles on "The Grimoire.""

That was it. That was my chance.

"About that. I wanted to talk to you about The Grimoire," I said. "I read your articles yesterday, and I thought they were super interesting. I was wondering if there was anything I could do to help you with them?"

I felt bad about lying through my teeth like that. Unfortunately, after years of practice ignoring Specters and deflecting questions, lying had become something that came to me as easily as breathing. Besides, there was a lot at stake. If I had to lie to save someone from a Specter, then so be it.

Amy's eyes lit up in response to my sweet nothings about The Grimoire. Despite her visible excitement, she attempted to play it cool.

"I'd appreciate the help," she said. "I was about to get lunch. Do you mind if we discuss it over at the dining hall?"

"That's fine with me," I replied.

#

I didn't live on campus, so I didn't eat at the campus dining hall much. After waiting in a cafeteria line and getting a grilled cheese that was almost completely charred on one side, I sat down and waited for Amy. I finally had a moment to gather my thoughts. I was still a little shaken by my encounter with that strange man, or Other, from earlier. The way he disappeared and couldn't be seen by Amy, I would've been genuinely surprised if he were remotely human.

What had Bennet said about Others? Something about supernatural beings that lived alongside us that usually can't be seen or perceived by normal people. That man seemed to fit that description perfectly. One thing in particular I found unnerving was that bit about me being famous in his "circle." What was that about?

I grimaced. *Sounds like I have more information I'll have to pry out from Bennet later. What a pain... I* thought to myself.

Amy sat down across from me, setting a plate with a grilled chicken sandwich and some French fries down on the table.

"Over here," a familiar, creepy voice cried.

The stuffed rabbit Poltergeist from earlier had finally appeared once more. It sat on the table next to her, swinging its legs back and forth like a hyperactive child. It stared intently at Amy, who remained blissfully unaware of the monster that was currently accompanying us.

"So you liked my articles on The Grimoire?" Amy asked.

"They were incredibly well researched," I said. "I also loved the passion you wrote with. Plus, I've always been super interested in stuff like ghosts and aliens."

It was a talent I loathed, but lying like this was a practiced skill I had mastered like someone would the piano.

"That means a lot to me," Amy said. "I work super hard on them. Hearing someone say they enjoyed them makes me happy."

"Oh, someone liked them, huh? Big whoop," the Poltergeist said in a pensive tone.

"What made you want to research this stuff?" I asked.

"I love researching urban legends," Amy replied, "and I've always wanted to meet a ghost, an alien, or anything like that. There's so much about them I want to learn and share with the rest of the world."

The Poltergeist hissed. "Liar," it said mockingly. "You just want to meet something weird because you're lonely and can't relate to anyone else."

Two girls walked past us.

"Aw, did the freak of Clover College give up UFO chasing and ghost hunting to chase boys?" one girl whispered.

"As if," the other replied in the same hushed tone. "He probably lost a bet with his friend or something and had to hang out with her because of it."

They continued along, quietly laughing to themselves. They probably thought they were being super sneaky, painfully unaware of how much their voices would carry when within a few feet of someone else, even in a crowded cafeteria.

"Don't worry about it," Amy said without prompting. "I'm used to it." She stared down at her plate, forcing a smile.

"Are you sure?" I asked with a genuine look of concern.

"All press is good press," she said. "They can say whatever they want. It doesn't bother me."

At that moment, the poltergeist got up and flipped Amy's plate into her lap, her half-eaten sandwich and fries spilling on her and onto the floor around her.

"Liar!" it cackled. "You want attention! You want to be special! But the things everyone says about you eat you away like cancer! You can't stand it!"

Amy sighed. "Another stroke of bad luck, probably from that curse I've been dealing with," she said half-jokingly.

Amy got out of her chair, kneeling on the floor to pick up the scattered contents of her lunch. I got up to help her.

"Thanks," she said.

"It's no big deal," I replied.

There was an awkward pause before Amy spoke again,

"I don't mean just helping pick up some spilled food," she said. "Thanks for being so nice to me."

The Poltergeist blew a raspberry as it watched both of us finish picking up the mess it had made. When the task was complete, we sat back down.

"Hey, Yuri," Amy said. "I'm going to this graveyard tomorrow to do some research about this urban legend I saw online…" Her shoulders stiffened as she looked away slightly. "Would you like to go with me?" she asked sheepishly.

I couldn't help but think back to my earlier reluctance to open up to Bennet when I first met him. I hated the thought of going to a graveyard, but…I knew it would make Amy happy, and that would be a big step in the process of befriending her and exorcising that Poltergeist. There wasn't any good reason to turn her down outside of my discomfort.

"Sure, it sounds fun," I said, with a carefully placed, nonchalant grin.

Amy's eyes lit up with both surprise and excitement.

"Thank you," she said.

I glanced back at the Poltergeist sitting on the table. Its chilling glare was fixed on me. The Poltergeist looked at me like a stray, feral dog, territorially guarding some meat scraps it had found.

CHAPTER 8

SECRETS AND DECEIT

I finally made it back to my apartment building that evening after attending classes. When I finished lunch with Amy, we made plans to meet up at Clover Hills Cemetery that upcoming Friday, and we made sure to exchange cell phone numbers before we left. I tossed my bag aside as I opened the door to my unit, locking the deadbolt behind me. I dropped my keys into a bowl I kept by the sink, and then I went to lie down on my bed. The day had been so eventful, I practically plopped myself on it like a trout out of water. I lay flat on my back as I waited for the tension to ease in my shoulders. Mustering what remained of my depleted motivation,   I took a deep breath before sitting back up in my bed. I pulled Bennet's charm out of my pocket and held up the leather string so that the green gemstone dangled in front of my face.

"You there, Bennet?" I called.

The charm, once again, began to give off its usual green glow.

"I am," Bennet replied.

"A lot's happened today," I said. "Before I tell you what happened with Amy, there's some stuff I wanted to talk to you about. I ran into someone on my way to campus today. I'm pretty sure he was an Other."

"Oh, what did he look like?" Bennet said.

"He was a creepy and intimidating man wearing a suit," I explained. "He said he was looking for me and warned me to stay away from you. He ended up disappearing the moment Amy came to talk to me, and he didn't come back at any point to elaborate on his vague warning."

Bennet groaned. "Ugh, that uptight numbskull doesn't have any boundaries," he complained.

"Do you know him?" I asked. "Is he an Other?"

"Yes," Bennet said. "He's a pretentious grim reaper who fancies himself a calculated professional. An honestly insufferable stick-in-the-mud type."

It felt safe to assume there was no love lost between Bennet and the strange man who'd called him an affront to the natural order.

"Is there a reason he wanted me to stay away from you?" I asked.

Bennet remained silent for a moment as he grappled for the right words. "I want to tell you, but..." he said, the hesitation audible in his voice.

"Is everything okay?" I asked.

"I'm sorry," Bennet said. "It's something I'm not incredibly proud of. I promise I will tell you everything someday, but for now…for now, I'd prefer to keep it close to my chest. All can say is that it's not something that you have to worry about. I promise."

I'd had conversations with Bennet quite a few times now, and this was the first time I'd heard him sound so serious. He was usually the type to push someone's buttons for the fun of it or put on the air of a cryptic sorcerer. That time, however, he almost sounded melancholy and pensive. Whatever his secret was, it must have been incredibly painful for him.

"Do you regret becoming my apprentice?" Bennet asked. "If you want to leave, I won't stop you. You can walk away like nothing happened anytime you like."

"Cut that out! You're not gonna rid of me that easy!"

I spat. "I've already seen too much to just go back to how things were before. Besides, I'm not just gonna sit by and watch Specters kill people. If I can see them, and there's something I can do to help, I'm gonna do it."

Bennet laughed weakly. "Well, aren't you devoted?" he said, quickly shifting back to his usual sanguine self.

"Now, about Amy: were you able to learn about anything troubling her? Any leads to what she may be repressing that attracted the Poltergeist in the first place?"

"I had lunch with her. The Poltergeist was there, too," I explained. "I asked her about some stuff she was writing about for a blog website, and every time she talked about it, the Poltergeist would interrupt and call her a liar."

"How so?" Bennet asked.

"Like, I asked why she was so interested in ghosts and aliens, and the Poltergeist shouted that she only wants to meet them because she's lonely and can't relate to people," I said. "At one point, some girls passed by, making fun of her. Amy tried to downplay it, but the Poltergeist freaked out a little bit and started shouting stuff about how she wants attention but won't admit that people making fun of her aren't getting under her skin."

"Sounds about right…" Bennet thought aloud. "The Poltergeist is calling her out on her inner feelings and sustaining itself on them. While Amy herself seems unaware of these emotions, it was their presence that attracted the Specter in the first place. Wanting to feel special and feeling isolated because of it—repressed feelings like those are more than enough to invite a Poltergeist to haunt you."

I bit my lip. I still had something else I needed to mention to him. "Hey, Bennet. Just before we talked yesterday, something weird happened," I said.

"What was it?" Bennet asked.

I fidgeted slightly. Being open and honest wasn't easy for me. Being emotionally vulnerable like this somehow felt even more terrifying than coming face to face with a Specter and narrowly avoiding death.

"When I was holding the flyer Amy gave me yesterday," I explained, "I felt a sharp pain in my head. I suddenly heard her voice. She shouted how she wanted someone to notice her and that she didn't want to be alone anymore. I've never experienced anything like that before."

"That power—" Bennet stammered.

"Is it something bad?"

"It's not. It's just a rare ability, is all," he said. "It caught me off guard."

"What is it?"

Bennet took a deep breath before he spoke, his tone almost somber and tired.

"It's called Resonance. It's an ability that allows someone to understand other people and Others in a way that transcends the boundaries of the soul. When they're near another person or a relic that person highly values, someone with Resonance can hear the true thoughts and feelings of that person. They can even experience that person's memories as if they lived and felt themself. It's an incredibly rare ability—even back during a time when mages were plentiful."

I was stunned. It was already crazy enough that I could see Specters. Being capable of something like what Bennet had just described surpassed any expectation of what I thought I was capable of.

Is it something I awoke to now that I'm not pushing everyone away anymore? I asked myself in deep thought. *Something that manifested now that I'm trying to come to terms with my curse?*

"The only other person I know of who ever had such an ability was my teacher—" Bennet thought aloud before cutting himself off. "Never mind. That part isn't important."

I got the sense I'd been close to hearing another bit of Bennet's past before he closed himself off again. Why was it that he always clammed up when the topic of his past came up? Did he not trust me? Or was it because he was that ashamed of himself? I hoped he would keep his promise and tell me someday. Bennet was annoying and insufferable most of the time, but he'd already helped me a lot. I wanted to help him, too… if I could.

#

Unceremoniously, the week passed by quickly. Soon it was Friday, and I was supposed to help with Amy's field research at Clover Hills Cemetery. After various text messages, we agreed to meet up there as soon as Amy finished classes that afternoon. Truth be told, I should've been in class as well, but I had other things on my mind.

That morning, I asked Bennet if I could practice exorcising Specters again. Considering I was about to head to a graveyard accompanied by someone being haunted by a Poltergeist, skipping class to practice exorcising Specters felt reasonable. I had visited Bennet at least once every day to train that week, but my practice still hadn't yielded any meaningful results. I was sitting on the usual purple couch in Bennet's home, staring down at the shriveled Ghoul from last time.

"Concentrate," Bennet said with a lit cigarette in his hand, "Envision what drives you forward, and let it create a warm light that drives away despair."

I held my hand over the cage, fixing my gaze on the shriveled Specter.

I won't let anyone else die.

That was my thought. A weak yellow glow flickered from my raised hand and vanished as quickly as it came.

"Damn it!" I cursed. "We've been at this for an hour straight now. Why can't I get it right?"

Bennet was reclining with his legs up on the couch while I practiced. "Come on now, frowning like that will cause wrinkles," he teased. "Besides, it's only been less than a week since you started learning how to exorcise Specters. Considering you're already creating faint sparks of magic, that's a tremendous amount of progress in such a short amount of time."

I scowled. "It's still not good enough," I said.

"An empire isn't built in a day, Yuri," Bennet said. "It's taken mages from far more accomplished backgrounds and bloodlines months to attain the progress you've made in a few days. Your potential is incredible, but you still need time and practice like everyone else."

I sighed, annoyed once again by the inescapable truth in Bennet's words.

"I'm sorry," I said. "I don't like graveyards at all. Plus, I have no idea what I'd do if that Poltergeist goes berserk like that giant crow monster out of Hell did."

Bennet took a puff from his cigarette, ashing it into a small ashtray next to him. "So that's what this is about," he said. "I can understand the part not liking graveyards. The lingering regrets of those who have departed, the sorrow of their grieving loved ones, and even the very thought of death that accompanies them are all quite foreboding. They're essentially breeding grounds for Specters."

I felt myself proverbially shrink, feeling dwarfed by the embarrassment brought on by admitting my fears out loud.

"Yeah," I replied, staring down at the floor. "Places like graveyards, hospitals, abandoned buildings that people said were haunted—all that crap. I always did everything I could to avoid them. I didn't know what they were at the time, but some of the scariest Specters I've seen always hung out around those places. It always baffled me why people actively chase ghosts, aliens, or monsters when seeing something like the real deal has me scared shitless all the time."

Bennet put out his cigarette. "That sounds on brand," he said. "It's common for Ghouls to be warped by public perception to resemble the urban legends they ultimately reinforce. It's another byproduct of the Malevolence Phenomenon. We humans are experts at creating make-believe monsters to terrify ourselves. Pity we lack the imagination and emotional clarity to make them go away."

Bennet stood up and went to stand behind me. He placed his hand on my shoulder and smiled at me as I looked up at him.

"Chin up," he said, "You don't have to shoulder everything on your own anymore. I said we'd be working with our 'client' together, didn't I?"

"You did," I replied, begrudgingly easing up.

"I'll be at the graveyard as well. I can deal with any unruly Specters and step in if Amy's Poltergeist goes berserk. If anything happens, all I need you to do is find the nearest door and run away with Amy to this house here on the Otherside. Poltergeists aren't super great at traveling between realities, so it will have a hard time chasing you both down if you're hiding in here."

The interaction felt painfully cheesy, but I appreciated the encouragement. It was reassuring if nothing else.

"Thanks," I replied.

"Care to sing my praises a little more?" Bennet teased.

"Now you just killed the mood entirely..." I groaned.

#

I practiced exorcising that Specter a few more times after that, but still had no success beyond faint sparks of magic. It was time to head for Clover Hills Cemetery. Bennet and I left The Otherside together, embarking from my apartment on foot to the cemetery.

"Remember what I told you earlier," Bennet said. "If anything happens, find the nearest door and escape to my house in the Otherside. It doesn't matter if it's a mausoleum door, a groundskeeper's shed, or anything else. As long as it's a solid door with no windows, it'll do. Even if it's locked, it'll open with that spell I taught you."

"Okay," I replied with a nod.

"Hey!" Amy called from the cemetery gate. "Over here!"

I could already feel Bennet's presence disappear as I walked towards Amy. Nothing more to do but face the task at hand.

Amy pulled a disposable camera out of her bag. "Smile," she chimed.

The camera's flash went off before I had a chance to realize she was taking a picture of me.

"What's with the camera?" I asked.

"It's for an urban legend I'm researching here," Amy explained. "Apparently, when you take photographs of the headstones here, you can see the spirit of the person it belongs to standing in front of them in the photos."

I think I heard something about that in a mystery novel I read a long time ago. Something about how the camera is supposed to capture what the naked eye can't see, like ghosts or spirits. However, most of the time, any apparitions that do appear in a photo can be easily explained by tricks of light or pareidolia.

"What is it you need me to do?" I asked.

"I want you to take pictures of the headstones with your phone," Amy said. "I wanted to make sure I got digital photos alongside ones developed from film to see if there was any impact on our ability to photograph ghosts."

I heard a familiar hissing off in the distance. "She's full of it, and she knows it," the Poltergeist goaded. It snickered while sitting on top of a nearby headstone, watching us like a spectator getting ready to throw peanuts at the players during a minor league baseball game.

"Easy enough," I said, putting on a brave face.

#

Clover Hills Cemetery was surprisingly large, with headstones and a few mausoleums spread out across a large parcel of land. The leaves in the trees nearby had started to turn to a warm orange, with the grass below dry and starting to yellow. A faint grey haze shrouded the cemetery and the sky. If I'd had to guess, it was probably because of the Ghouls and the lingering despair that hung around there.

I hated every second of being at that cemetery. The odor the Specters gave off was weak, but it pervaded the entire graveyard. As I passed by various headstones, I could see translucent eyes and tendrils rise from them. They were small fry Specters—Ghouls, as Bennet called them. I was willing to bet they were waiting for someone vulnerable to haunt.

I shuddered. *Ugh, these things are so gross...* I thought to myself in disgust.

The very atmosphere felt mildly oppressive. It was a feeling similar to trying to wade through knee-deep water that was slimy and scummy. That heaviness, for better or worse, was lost on Amy. She already marched forth like a soldier on a mission, taking photos of nearby headstones with the disposable camera she'd brought with her. I made sure to take note of the various mausoleums and the storage shed near the entrance on the off chance I needed to use them to escape with her at a moment's notice.

As I passed by a headstone, a tendril with an eye attached to it rose from the grave like a wildflower from another planet. The transparent Ghoul made direct eye contact with me and blinked a few times. After I thought about it, I realized that it never occurred to me to try to take a picture of a Specter before. Maybe there was some truth to the urban legend after all.

I pulled out my phone and opened up the camera app, taking a picture of the Ghoul in front of me as it gently swayed with the breeze. Sure enough, the picture my phone took showed nothing out of the ordinary—just a simple image of a faded headstone in a mundane reality. There was no faint, ominous haze made of human despair that filled the sky or an eerie apparition looking to prey upon humans. It was a picture from a world where no supernatural monsters lurked in the shadows. A picture that showcased a banal reality as everyone else saw it.

"Should've seen that coming…" I quietly muttered to myself.

Putting my phone back in my pocket, I found a nearby bench to sit on as I watched Amy carry on with her survey. She remained laser-focused as she took pictures of each headstone one by one, methodically examining each marker and reading the names written on them before carefully aiming her disposable camera and taking a picture. I sat on the bench, twiddling my thumbs as she carried on.

"Still at it, aren't you? Don't you know you're wasting your time?" the Poltergeist taunted.

The Poltergeist laughed at Amy while sitting in a nearby tree. It left a bitter taste in my mouth. I felt bad for Amy. The Poltergeist, the strangers on the internet, even people at our college laughed at her like hecklers in the cheap seats of a theatre. Every time, she played it off, unaware that every snide comment was slowly eating away at her and making the Poltergeist stronger.

I got up from the bench. "Hey, Amy?" I asked while approaching her, "Why do you try so hard at this?"

"What do you mean?" she asked.

"I mean, doesn't it bother you?" I asked. "People in your comments section making fun of you, or the assholes on campus who gossip behind your back?"

Amy looked away. "All press is good pre—"

"But doesn't that still bother you?" I interrupted.

The whistling of the wind only emphasized the weight of my question.

"What does it matter?" Amy asked.

I clenched my fists. "Because this stuff is stupid—" I said before immediately cutting myself off.

I had messed up. I got impulsive and didn't think about what I was doing all the way through. Amy started tearing up.

"Were you just lying to me this entire time?" she shouted. "Do you think I'm a loon like everyone else?"

My words failed me. She was right; I wasn't any better. I'd lied to her and judged her behind her back. I did all of this despite saying I wanted to save her. I was arrogant.

"I knew it," Amy muttered to herself. "I thought I finally met someone who understood."

The sky darkened as a foul wind started to pick up.

"I'm so stupid," Amy said. "I shouldn't have gotten my hopes up."

The Poltergeist laughed maniacally. "That's right!" it cackled, its voice tumbling down to a distorted, guttural growl as it did. "You're just a dumb girl no one could ever understand or care about! Did you think that someone could understand you, let alone care about you? Pathetic!"

I stood paralyzed as my clumsy attempts to open Amy's eyes and save her from herself blew up in my face spectacularly.

CHAPTER 9

HONEST CONVERSATIONS

The very atmosphere in the graveyard started to change. A sense of dread filled the air, which made it feel thin and hard to breathe. Even the small-fry Ghouls that resided there were making themselves scarce.

The Poltergeist cackled at us, reveling in Amy's despair, its voice now booming and distorted like that of a terrifying demon.

"Don't you get it yet?" it said. "Everybody hates you! You are alone!"

Its head started to twitch before tearing completely like that of a broken stuffed animal. A black, smoke-like sludge oozed out.

"I'm sorry for wasting your time," Amy said coldly. "I should have known better than to think anyone could understand me."

"That's right!" the Poltergeist cried. "You're a burden! A waste of space!"

The sludge piled and congealed as it slowly began to form a feral beast. Large and bulging, the only reason it vaguely resembled a rabbit was because of the floppy ears on top of its head. It dwarfed Amy and me.

This felt just like before, when the other Poltergeist had attacked me. It was like time itself had stopped in mid-motion. Amy now stood frozen with the rest of the world around us.

"Now you've done it…" Bennet called.

He appeared behind us, his messy red hair dancing dramatically in the wind.

"Bennet!" I called. "I'm so sorry, I just wanted to help her understand what she was feeling. I didn't think it'd end up like this!"

"Back off, humans!" the Poltergeist roared. "That girl's soul is mine!"

Bennet scoffed. "Too late for regrets now, I'm afraid," he said. "Focus on what we can still do to make the situation better. You remember what I told you earlier, yes?"

I nodded, pulling myself together.

"Right! I'm on it!" I said, springing into action.

Bennet smirked. "Good, I'll buy you some time," he said, directing his attention to the berserk Poltergeist.

Before I could even move, the Poltergeist lunged forward at me with all its might. Bennet stepped in front of me.

"Not so fast!" he shouted.

A yellow barrier appeared before him, repelling the Poltergeist and launching it into a nearby mausoleum.

"If you want that girl's soul, you'll have to go through me!" Bennet declared. "Try and entertain me at least a little bit, k?"

I rushed toward Amy, grabbing her arm. The very moment I touched her, she came back to her senses.

"Wait, where am I?" she said. "What's going on, Yuri?"

Her eyes finally fell upon the Poltergeist that had been haunting her all this time, widening in terror.

"What is that thing?" she screamed.

Amy trembled, standing frozen in terror.

"I'll explain later!" I shouted.

Holding tight to Amy's arm, I ran towards the groundkeeper's shed by the cemetery gate.

"Yuri! Watch out!" Bennet called.

At that moment, a headstone barreled at Amy and me. I tackled her to the ground, narrowly avoiding what would have been certain death. The headstone shattered off in the distance. Amy stared in terror and confusion as I helped her back up. I grabbed her arm once more and sprinted towards the storage shed. I frantically invoked the motions needed, my knuckles banging loudly as I knocked twice on the door. My heart was racing. I was breathing heavily. I couldn't concentrate; the images in my mind were blurring in a chaotic, panicked, hot mess. I was just as scared as Amy when I invoked the spell.

"I journey to the Otherside!" I cried.

I opened the shed door. Without even thinking, I pulled Amy inside, slamming the door shut behind us. I took heavy breaths, trying to calm myself down.

"Where are we?" Amy asked.

I finally came to my senses. Amy and I stood in a large field of flowers that looked like they came out of the pages of a storybook. The sky was a warm pink, with sepia-toned clouds that looked like they'd been painted on the heavens with high-end oil paint on canvas. Behind us stood a peculiar oak door and frame, isolated in the field of brightly colored flowers.

"Damn it…" I muttered under my breath.

I'd been so panicked that I didn't picture Bennet's cottage when I invoked the spell. I pulled the charm from my pocket, holding it by the string so that the green gem was suspended in front of my face.

"Bennet!" I called. "Bennet! Can you hear me?"

There was no response.

"Yuri!" Amy said with a shout, her patience now completely nonexistent. "Tell me what the hell is going on! Now! Where are we? And what the hell was that monster?"

I took a deep breath. "I'm sorry," I said. "I'll tell you everything."

I looked up at the bright pink sky above us.

"This is a place called the Otherside," I explained. "I'm still trying to wrap my head around it, but it's basically like a world parallel to the one we live in."

"Another world?"

"Yeah…"

I clenched my fists, bracing myself to confess the thing I'd kept from others for years, until I'd met Bennet.

"I can see these things called Specters," I said. "I didn't know what they're called or what they are until a few days ago. They're basically like ghosts that are attracted to human despair. That monster was a Specter, a Poltergeist drawn to repressed emotions, that was haunting you. The man fighting it right now is Bennet. He's a mage I met a few days ago who knows how to exorcise them. I had a Specter haunting me, too, until recently. He saved me when it went berserk."

Amy looked around the field of flowers and the bright pink sky above us. I could have only imagined the kind of fear or confusion she was feeling.

"You're not lying, are you?" she said, dumbfounded. "This feels all too real to be some kind of prank or a wild dream I'm having."

I still couldn't bring myself to look at Amy because of my guilt.

"I'm sorry about lying to you earlier. Not just about this, but about liking your blog and stuff. The truth is that urban legends about monsters and the paranormal scare the crap out of me. The things I see every day make me feel like I'm living a god damn ghost story, so I can't stand them," I said.

"Then why did you lie to me?" Amy asked.

I stared down at the ground. I couldn't bring myself to look at her. The thought of looking into Amy's eyes felt terrifying and humiliating. Everything I'd done up to that point had been nothing but shameful.

"I…" I stammered as I felt my throat choke up. "I… I watched my mom die because of a Specter… Bennet's been teaching me about them since he saved me the other day. When I met you at the convenience store last weekend, I saw that Specter try to kill you there as well. I'm borderline useless fighting Specters and just about everything else. I wasn't able to do anything to help my mom back then, and I'm just as powerless now. Despite that, I know I wouldn't be able to live with myself if I let a Specter kill someone again. I was prepared to lie and say anything I needed to get closer to you, so I could stop it. I knew you wouldn't have believed me if I told you about that Poltergeist otherwise. I'm sorry. I didn't mean to hurt you."

"Yuri..." Amy said quietly, audibly, and understandably stunned.

We remained speechless, both of us unsure of what to say. The silence lingered for what felt like an eternity before Amy finally asked the one question I dreaded more than anything.

"So what now?" she asked.

I ruffled the hair at the side of my head as I desperately tried to gather my thoughts. "We can't just go back through that door," I said. "We'll end up back at the cemetery where Bennet is fighting that Specter. I was supposed to take you to a house where Bennet lives, but I panicked, screwed up, and took us God knows where in the Otherside."

I sat down, the weight and fatigue of these last few minutes finally setting in.

"Bennet said if something like this were to happen, to just stay put," I said before holding up the charm. "As long as I have this, he should be able to track us down. Sooner or later, anyway."

Amy quietly sat down next to me.

"Okay," she said.

I took deep breaths, trying to calm my anxious mind.

I couldn't afford to lose my cool.

#

Amy and I sat in the field of flowers, waiting and brooding. A few minutes could have passed, or it could have very well been a few hours; there was no way for us to tell for sure. I tried to check my phone's clock at one point, but it had shut down completely, and Amy's watch also proved to be equally useless. It felt safe to assume standard electronic devices didn't work in the Otherside. They might as well have been paperweights in our current situation. Unable to even keep track of time, each moment Amy and I waited felt like agony. The radio silence from Bennet made it all the worse. I clutched onto the charm he lent me, praying that he would reach out any moment.

I remained on high alert, my ears pricked for even the slightest change in sound, ready to grab Amy and run at a moment's notice if I had to. The tension I felt was jarring in contrast to the pastel flowers that surrounded us. The warmth and bright colors painted an entirely different emotional atmosphere.

"Look! Humans!" a small, squeaky voice called.

Amy and I leaped to our feet upon hearing the voice.

"It's been so long since this one has seen humans," another small voice said.

"It's been at least eighty moons since this one last saw a human."

"How did the humans get here?"

Amy and I looked around frantically, trying to find the source of the voices. It felt like they'd surrounded us.

Something small flew out of the flowers and stopped within an inch of my face. The creature was small, green, and vaguely humanoid. It had bright, patterned wings that fluttered like those of a dragonfly and large black eyes that sparkled with curiosity.

"What's this human boy called?" the creature said.

"Yuri," I replied, still stunned by this creature's sudden appearance.

"Yur-REE!" the creature said, stumbling on the syllables like it was a foreign language.

The creature flew into Amy's face next. "And what's this human girl called?" it asked.

"Amy," she replied, startled and confused.

"Aim-EE," another creature parroted back.

Another similar creature flew out of the flowers. "Humans always have the strangest names," it said.

"What are you?" I asked.

Two more creatures flew out from the flowers below.

"These ones are pixies!" the first cheered.

"Why are Aim-EE and Yur-REE here?" the second asked.

Amy defensively raised her hands. "We wandered here by mistake," she said. "We don't mean any trouble."

"We're just waiting to hear back from a friend," I said while nervously nodding.

More pixies started to fly out of the flowers.

"It's been so long since these ones have seen humans!"

"These ones want to play!"

My heart raced a little bit as my fight or flight instinct kicked in. "I'm sorry," I replied frantically, "But we'll be heading out of here anytime now."

"Come on! Play with these ones!" another pixie exclaimed.

Amy tightly gripped my wrist. "Yuri, I'm scared," she said softly.

The pixies swarmed us, slowly closing in, speaking in unison as they approached.

"Play with these ones," they echoed in unison, "Forever and ever…"

"Now now, little ones," a woman's voice called, "I know you love to play, but try to be considerate of others."

Amy and I were startled by the sudden sight of a middle-aged woman standing a small distance away in the flowers. She had olive-toned skin and curly, sandy brown hair that she had tied into a messy bun on the side of her head. She wore a long-sleeved dress with a knee-length skirt, all mismatched patterns and bright neon purples and yellows, with a pair of brown leather boots.

"That boy is the apprentice of Bennet Grey," she said. "I can only imagine how poorly he'd react if you played too roughly with him and his companion."

"That human belongs to Bennie?" a pixie asked.

"When Bennie gets mad, things get really scary!" another pixie cried.

"This one is sorry!" yet another exclaimed.

The pixies, in quick succession, retreated to the flowers from which they'd emerged, disappearing as suddenly as they appeared. For the time being, Amy and I were safe.

"I do apologize for the pixies," the woman said. "Their desire to play is as genuine as it gets, but they don't quite comprehend how fragile humans are compared to Others."

Amy bowed her head to the woman. "Thanks a million for saving us!" she said. "I thought we were toast…"

"Think nothing of it, Amy," the woman replied.

Amy and I looked at each other in stunned confusion and apprehension.

"How did you know her name?" I asked.

The woman chuckled. "I'm sorry," she said, "I haven't properly introduced myself yet. My name is Lucia, but I am also known as the Observer."

"The Observer? What's that?" Amy asked.

Lucia looked us up and down.

"Yuri Weissman. Amy LeBlanc," she said. "You both escaped here after fleeing from a Poltergeist that was haunting Amy and had gone berserk. The one who calls himself Bennet Grey is currently in the process of subduing the Poltergeist, but when you tried to escape, you both ended up here by mistake. Is that correct?"

I stared at Lucia, stunned. "Who—what are you?" I asked.

"I am the Observer," Lucia said. "I watch over all humans and Others, recording the lives that they live. I would be unfit for my station if I couldn't observe simple events as those, would I?"

"Long time, no see, Lucia," Bennet's voice called.

He emerged from the doorway that led us here, closing it behind him.

"Bennet!" I called, "Are you okay?"

"I've handled far worse than that," he scoffed, "though I am flattered you're so concerned about me."

As usual, Bennett managed to find a way to get under my skin, but at least he hadn't gotten hurt because of me. Lucia gently clasped her hands at her waist.

"It's been far too long, Bennett," she said.

Amy approached him. "Thank you for saving me," Amy said, still flustered by his sudden appearance.

"You flatter me, madame," Bennet said playfully. "But I'm afraid the job is still far from done."

He snapped his fingers with a dramatic flourish. Amy and I recoiled backward as the berserk Poltergeist from before appeared in front of us. It was limp and taking slow and shallow breaths, beaten and bruised like a wounded animal. It was bound by a series of what looked like glowing ropes made of solid light.

"I assume Yuri already told you about the beast's true nature, yes?" Bennet said.

Amy silently nodded, still visibly terrified by the monster slumped on the ground in front of us.

"Good, that saves us some time then," Bennet replied. "That monster is bound to feelings deep in your heart that you're denying. It will never truly be slain until you accept those feelings."

Amy stood next to me, visibly trembling.

"Think about it nice and hard," Bennet said, "You must surely be starting to realize what it is that you've denied in your heart for so long."

Amy looked like a deer caught in the headlights, frozen and paralyzed by fear and uncertainty. Who wouldn't have been in a situation like this? The sight of it made me ache. Was I supposed to say something? What, though? It was possible I could end up making everything worse again. What would happen if I said something stupid? What if I said something made the situation worse? I had to say *something*, though... right? I felt like I owed Amy that much at least.

"It's okay," I said. "It's hard and scary."

Amy met my gaze.

"I struggled with it too," I said. "Accepting a truth I tried desperately to ignore for years. I'm still struggling… But if you want to be free from this pain, if you don't want it to rule your life anymore, the only way to heal is to face that truth head-on."

Amy nodded. She stepped towards the beast, gently kneeling beside it.

"I think I get it now," she said. "It was a part of me I couldn't accept. I felt so lonely. I was afraid of getting rejected, and I wanted so badly to feel special that I chased after ghost stories and urban legends to escape from it all." The Poltergeist started to emit a warm yellow glow.

"I don't want to run away from everyone anymore."

The beast became a bright light, radiating gentle warmth as it scattered like fireflies to the wind. The Specter was no more.

"I never thought I'd see a day when you took on an apprentice, Bennet," Lucia said.

He shrugged. "I never thought I would either," he said playfully. "But what can I say? This one's piqued my interest. He's clumsy and rough around the edges, but he has a lot of potential."

"Your teacher would be proud," Lucia said.

Bennet's shoulders stiffened at the comment, but he didn't let his devil-may-care grin break. "I like to think he would be as well," Bennet said. "But that's a conversation for another time."

He gestured with his hand to Amy and me. "These two have been through a lot already," he said. "It's time I get them back to the Nearside and let them get some well-deserved rest."

Lucia curtsied. "Farewell for now, then," she said. "Please, take care."

#

Amy, Bennet, and I emerged from the storage shed in Clover Hills Cemetery. Our surroundings had been restored to the state they'd been in before the Poltergeist went berserk. Every headstone was intact, and only a mild sense of unease filled the air as the Ghouls that had fled from the Poltergeist returned. The cemetery had effectively been reset. Bennet escorted Amy and me to the main gate.

"I'm sorry again about everything," I said.

Amy shook her head. "It's okay," she said. "I'm sorry about the mess I caused as well."

"Do you need Yuri to walk you home?" Bennet asked. "I'll be okay. My dorm isn't too far from here," Amy said. "I'm tired as all get out, but my head feels the clearest it's been in a long time."

"I'm glad," Bennet said. "Try to take it easy for a little while, okay?"

"I will," Amy replied.

She started to leave for her dorm.

"Bye," I called awkwardly.

Amy turned around. "Thank you for everything, Yuri!" she called. "I'll see you later."

And with that, Amy marched off. I couldn't tell if she was putting on a brave face or not, but the Poltergeist that had haunted her was nowhere to be seen. It looked like Bennet and I had completed what we set out to do.

"Care for a walk?" Bennet asked.

"I don't get to say 'no' here, do I?" I said, rolling my eyes.

"You're a quick learner," he replied.

#

The sun was starting to set as Bennet and I journeyed back to my apartment, the sky a marmalade orange. We'd traversed a few blocks without saying a word. His silence was punctuated only by the occasional sound of wind rustling leaves in nearby trees or of cars that periodically passed us by. Bennet sauntered next to me, slouching slightly, hands in his pockets. Just as I thought we'd go the entire time without so much as saying a word to each other, he finally spoke up.

"You did a good job today," he said.

I frowned. "I don't feel like I did," I replied.

"Amy's safe, and the Poltergeist that haunted her got exorcised. That feels like a job well done to me," Bennet said.

"You were the one to subdue that Poltergeist," I retorted, "Amy was the one who ultimately made it disappear. Everything I did made the whole situation worse."

"You set out to complete a task, and even if you made mistakes and messed up, the fact of the matter is that you accomplished what you set out to do. You made your will a reality. It's more than a lot of people can say, Yuri," Bennet said.

He stretched out his right arm over his head, yawning softly.

"Besides, you were just as instrumental in helping Amy," he said. "You saved her from that Poltergeist on two different occasions, and you helped her come to grips with her feelings when she was struggling to do so in the end. Yes, mistakes were made, but you survived, and you can learn from them."

I sighed. "I got lucky too," I said. "Lucia was the one who ultimately saved Amy and me when I got both of us stranded on the Otherside. I'm not sure what I would have done about those pixies."

"Let me guess. Those pixies wanted to play, and then high-tailed it when Lucia mentioned that you were my student," Bennet said. He shook his head. "Classic Lucia," he muttered.

After a moment, Bennet gave a weary sigh.

"I'm going to have to teach you more about Others in case something like that happens again," he groaned. "It was a good thing they heeded her warning the way they did. Had they not, you and Amy would have fared much worse, and Lucia wouldn't have been able to do anything about it."

I tried not to picture what would have happened if the alternative scenario Bennet proposed had been the one to play out.

"It also saves me the trouble of having to pluck the wings off some troublesome pixies later," he added.

"Is that what she meant by being an Observer or whatever?" I asked.

Bennet's eyes narrowed, his expression now more serious.

"In a sense," he said, "Lucia is a powerful being who can't directly interfere with the lives of living things under normal circumstances. She can only inform and advise at best."

"What exactly is she?" I asked, a little concerned.

"There are two powerful beings that reside in the Otherside," Bennet explained. "Lucia is the Observer, and that annoying grim reaper you met the other day is the Collector. They are cosmic entities who essentially preside over life and death."

"Cosmic entities," I echoed, visibly stunned. "Like gods?"

Fallen leaves rustled against the sidewalk as we walked.

"They're similar, but they're not real gods as you would know them," Bennet explained. "They're more like abstract concepts given human form. The Observer was formed from humanity's desire to preserve knowledge for future generations. She records the lives of humans and Others from the day they are born until the day they die. The Collector, on the other hand, is formed from humanity's instinct to fear and prepare for death. He records the names of those who die, collects data surrounding their final moments, and watches over their souls as they return to the Farside so they can eventually be reborn anew. That insufferable harbinger of death only ever gets directly involved in the world's affairs when it comes to preserving the natural order."

I had no idea what to make of the new information I had just learned, but the feeling of being confused by unusual cosmic truths didn't feel as terrifying as it had before. Maybe I was just getting desensitized to the chaos of it all. There was so much I still didn't know about the world, and I felt like I'd never know the whole truth for sure. That said, all I could do was keep moving forward, regardless of whatever lay ahead.

Bennet stopped in his tracks. "Yuri," he said. "I need you to promise me something."

He frowned, his expression troubled. I couldn't help but feel a subtle sense of urgency and desperation in his request.

"What is it?" I asked.

Bennet stared off into the sunset, unable to look at me as he spoke.

"If something ever happens to me. I want you to seek out Lucia," he said.

This was probably the most emotionally vulnerable I'd seen Bennet so far. Weirdly, it was reassuring. It helped remind me that this enigmatic mage who prattled on about cosmic truths like they were bland trivia was still a person with his own fears and insecurities deep down.

"Promise me," Bennet said once more.

I didn't understand why Bennet had suddenly brought this up, but it was clearly very important to him.

"I promise," I replied.

Bennet smiled.

"Thank you," he said.

#

After that exchange, Bennet and I didn't talk at all until we arrived at my apartment building. When we got there, he saw me off before he went to return to the Otherside. When I stepped into my apartment, my body almost felt as heavy as a sack of bricks. I hadn't ever felt this physically tired. I fell on my bed like it was pulling me with a magnetic force.

I had so many questions buzzing in my head. Bennet was one giant enigma. He had intimate knowledge of cosmic truths that many could barely dream of and revealed them ever so casually. He was well acquainted with beings that supposedly preside over life and death, and even Others seemed to dread the idea of needlessly crossing him. There was also something from his past that he was deeply ashamed of. In short, Bennet Grey was annoying, overly cryptic, and a slob who smoked way too much. Despite all of that, I somehow still can't help but trust him.

My phone buzzed with a text message. It was from Amy. *Hey, do you feel like meeting up to get lunch or something tomorrow?*

I couldn't help but crack a dumb grin. Is this what it felt like to have a friend? I can't say that I hated the feeling.

Sure, that sounds fun, I texted back.

I closed my eyes and fell asleep almost instantly, blissfully unaware of the upcoming trials and tribulations I would come to face over the coming year.

CHAPTER 10

THE DETECTIVE'S REQUEST

One night when I was fourteen years old, I remember sitting and having dinner with my mom. She had dark shadows under her eyes, and she was exhausted as all get out. A Specter shaped like a small black bird was perched on her shoulder. It had come and gone a lot while I was growing up, but by the time I started high school, it wouldn't ever leave her side. We quietly ate a stir-fry she made that evening.

"Are things going well at school?" my mom asked.

"They're going fine," I said, not looking up from my bowl.

"Have you thought about joining any clubs or anything?" my mom asked.

"No," I replied.

The spectral canary on her shoulder tilted its head.

"This boy's a burden on you," it hissed. "He leeches off of you and offers nothing in return."

I didn't acknowledge or even look in the direction of the Specter. I had grown so accustomed to tuning them out by then. After all, at that time, they were only supposed to be figments of my imagination.

"Are you at least making friends?" my mom asked.

"I'm okay on my own," I replied.

"Don't you wish this boy were the one who died?" the bird said. "He should have been the one who died over your beloved Derek."

I set down my fork.

"Are you not feeling well?" my mom asked.

"I'm not hungry," I replied. "Sorry."

"Don't you want to kill him? It would feel so satisfying," the bird urged. "You would finally be free from these ties that bind you."

I maintained a straight face, numbing myself to the bird's advocacy for my death. "I'm going to go to bed for the night," I said.

"Okay…" my mom replied.

My mom's smile was gentle, but it couldn't conceal the worry and pain she felt. I didn't know what Specters were at the time, but I always felt deep down that my mom had come to resent me. However, had I known what was going to happen—that she would take her own life because of the Specter haunting her— I would have done anything to save her.

Why didn't I do anything? Why did I push her away like that?

That's what I asked myself over and over all these years. That was the regret I always carried with me. That mistake was the one that haunted me to this very day.

#

It had been a month and a half since my chance encounter with Bennet. Almost every day, I visited Bennet's cottage in the Otherside whenever I finished class. It had taken a lot of time and effort, but I finally managed to make some progress with my training under his instruction. I'd gotten to a point where I could exorcise the weak ghouls he prepared for me. Despite Bennet's praises and his assurance that I was mastering advanced magic faster than any normal mage would, I still dreaded the idea of facing a Specter that was fighting to kill. As my days whittled by, mid-September gave way to October, and time continued marching onward to mid-November. Midterms had come and gone. Only a few weeks remained before my final exams and the end of the semester.

I sat across from Amy at a small table in a coffee shop. Textbooks, flashcards, and notebooks were scattered across the table's surface. Amy quizzed me on my course material.

"What is learned helplessness?" she asked, reading from my study guide.

"Learned helplessness is a mental state where someone is conditioned to believe they have no control over a situation, even when given the opportunities and power to affect it directly," I replied.

"Very well put," Amy said.

She set the study guide in her hand down on the table before picking up the iced coffee she had been chipping away at during our study session.

"I'm not sure why you asked me to help you study," she said jokingly. "You already seem like you know everything that's going to be on your final psych exam."

I shrugged. "It's not so much that I need help understanding the material as I need someone to keep me from slacking off," I said.
"I find this stuff so dry and boring. I never get anything done when I'm alone at my apartment."

"You still haven't declared a major, right?" Amy asked.

"Yep," I replied.

"Do you have any long-term plans or any idea what you might want to study next fall?"

"Nope," I replied once more.

Amy chuckled. "Well, that was direct.".

I leaned back in my chair, playing with a lock of my hair as I simmered in painful nostalgia.

"I didn't put much thought into college, honestly," I said. "After my mom died, I was sent to stay with my aunt, uncle, and grandma. We aren't exactly on great terms, and doing the college thing was the most convenient way to get the hell out of there."

"Why aren't you guys on good terms?" Amy asked.

"They blamed me for my mom's death," I said.

Amy froze for a moment.

"That's awful!" she exclaimed. "I'm sorry they treated you like that."

I leaned forward, placing my elbow on the table and resting my head in my hand.

"It's okay. Honestly. I don't hold it against them at all," I said. "I get it. After everything that happened, I blame me too."

I sighed, sitting back up in my seat.

"But I'm working on it," I said. "I'm hoping that by helping Bennet, I can get some answers and find some way to make up for it. Maybe then I'll be able to forgive myself."

"Yuri, I—" Amy stammered.

"It's fine," I said, cutting her off. "I shouldn't have brought something so heavy up out of the blue like that. Besides, I need to focus on studying right now. I'm gonna be in a world of hurt if I end up flunking out because I moped around over the past instead of studying."

Amy gave me a sullen look, clearly hesitant to change the topic.

"Okay..." she finally relented, halfheartedly, picking up my study guide once more.

I appreciated being able to open up to Amy like this. It was something I never got to do before. It almost felt alien to me. Not having to keep someone at an arm's length like I always did... As strange as this sensation was, I still found it liberating.

I'd made sure to keep in touch with Amy after everything that happened with the Poltergeist and our misadventure to the Otherside. She was even nice enough to help keep me honest with my schoolwork and quiz me on my various class materials. That said, there were still a few things I needed to figure out on my own. I didn't feel comfortable talking about my feelings with Amy when I didn't even understand what my heart was saying, or where the hell my head was at.

As I mentally prepared myself to study once more, I felt a sudden warmth radiate from Bennet's charm in my pocket.

"Yuri," his voice echoed from the stone. "I'm outside. As soon as you're ready, I need you to come with me to meet a contact."

I got out of my seat, putting on my windbreaker as I stood up.

"Sorry, Amy," I said. "Bennet just called. I'm pretty sure he needs my help with a job."

"Calling you telepathically with that strange stone tied to a string again?" she asked playfully.

"The truth is always stranger than fiction, believe or not," I dryly mused.

Amy laughed. "Yeah, I don't doubt it. Honestly, I saw that weird Otherside place firsthand, and I still have a hard time wrapping my brain around it. Hearing another person's voice through a stone sounds way more plausible in comparison."

I smirked. "Good to know I'm not crazy then."

I put my things away in my book bag, slinging it over my shoulder as I prepared to leave.

"I'll see you later. Thanks again for all the help," I said.

"No problem," Amy replied. "Stay safe out there, and say hi to Bennet for me, alright?"

"Will do," I remarked with a playful nod before waving goodbye.

#

When I exited the coffeeshop, I found Bennet sitting at a nearby bench. He wore a heavy, charcoal grey trench coat with an emerald green scarf around his neck.

"So where's this contact you wanted me to meet?" I asked.

"Come on," he said, standing up and gesturing with his hand to follow. "Let's walk and talk."

I carefully tailed Bennet down the sidewalk, struggling to keep up with his brisk pace.

"In a hurry?" I asked.

"Something like that," Bennet said. "My contact has a busy schedule, and I'd rather not keep him waiting."

"What do you mean?" I asked.

Bennet and I continued to hike up the sidewalk.

"You remember how I told you when we first met that one of my primary roles as a mage was to maintain the world's balance?" Bennet said.

"Yeah," I replied. "Are we meeting with an Other?"

123

"No, this contact is human," he said. "We agreed to meet at a nearby paid parking garage."

I furrowed my brow in confusion. "Is he a mage or something?" I asked.

"Nope. He's a homicide detective," Bennet said.

"So, how does a meeting with a homicide detective help keep the world's balance?"

Bennet came to an abrupt halt. "The Otherside is intrinsically linked to our world, the Nearside," he said. "They are like two sides of the same coin. While Malevolence plagues people here in the form of Specters, it has a far more sinister effect in the Otherside."

I grimaced. "Ugh, that doesn't sound creepy and cryptic at all," I sarcastically quipped.

Bennet rolled his eyes at my passive aggression. "The cosmic energy, Malevolence, manifests in our world like a grey haze where human despair is heavily concentrated," he explained. "However, that excess in Malevolence also impacts the Otherside. The border between mind and reality is far thinner there. In the Otherside, Malevolence acts more like a blight. It's a miasma that corrodes everything in its path if it's not purified. Because of the Otherside's proximity to the Farside, it could easily damage the very cycle of death and rebirth itself, potentially ending all life as we know it."

I shuddered, picturing the black ooze I had seen from Specters so many times and imagining it eating away at the world like dark matter.

"So, when we helped Amy a few months ago…did that help preserve balance on the Otherside?" I asked.

"That was mainly for your benefit," Bennet said casually. "Come on. We need to get going."

Bennet marched onward.

"The Specter was a potentially deadly nuisance for Amy, yes," he said. "But in the grand scheme of things, it was ultimately a small fry. I figured it would be best to help ease you into this line of work by encouraging you to help someone of your own free will."

"So what is it you usually do?" I asked.

"I take on requests and cases," Bennet said. "People and Others come to me with problems, usually involving Specters or Malevolence, that no one else can solve. I've developed contacts both in the Nearside and on the Otherside, so I can properly fulfill my duty. The detective we're about to meet usually reaches out when he needs help with criminals with some connection to the supernatural. Stuff human law enforcement and the like would be in way over their heads trying to handle."

I wasn't sure how to feel about all of this. While I had been studying how to purify Specters with Bennet for the better part of a month and a half, I never once thought about the potential magnitude of what he was tasked with handling. It at least explained why almost every Other I encountered so far either respected him or dreaded the idea of crossing him.

#

Bennet and I arrived at the parking garage where the detective had agreed to meet. It was a small three-story structure that felt cramped and uninviting, not at all helped by the cold November air that pervaded the area.

I shivered, wishing I had brought a heavier jacket than the light windbreaker I was currently wearing.

Bennet led me to the second floor, and after quickly scouring the area, we happened upon a man who was standing outside a black SUV. He was on the slightly older side, probably in his late forties or early fifties, with dark hair and a heavy black parka.

"Linny," Bennet greeted playfully, his tone almost pedantic.

"It's Detective Linebeck," the man said with a scowl.

"Oh, come on now," Bennet replied. "I remember when you were just a fresh-faced boy with dreams about going to the police academy."

"And you haven't changed a bit…" Detective Linebeck said.

He took notice of me and eyed me up and down, his gaze probing and intimidating. He reminded me of the hard-boiled detective type characters I'd seen in novels or TV crime dramas.

"Hi," I greeted nervously.

"Who's he?" Detective Linebeck said, his tone cold.

"For all intents and purposes, he's my assistant," Bennet said. "You can trust him, I assure you."

Detective Linebeck's posture relaxed, albeit begrudgingly. He placed his hands in the pockets of his parka, slouching slightly.

"You only ever come calling when you have some scary kingpin or serial killer that needs dealing with," Bennet said. "Care to treat me to lunch first?"

"Not happening," Detective Linebeck replied.

"Oh, so cold. I thought we were friends," the mage said with a sarcastic pout.

"Cut the crap."

Bennet mockingly threw his hands in the air in defeat. "Very well," he said. "What depraved criminal will I be taking care of for you this time?"

Detective Linebeck looked like he was straining not to burst a blood vessel in his skull. I suspected that he only ever consulted with Bennet as a last resort. I could practically see his blood pressure rising as he endured Bennet being…well, Bennet.

"You have a knack for being a pain in the ass," Detective Linebeck complained. He gave me a stone-cold glare. "What I'm about to say doesn't get repeated to anyone, got it?"

I nodded slowly in response, silenced by the intensity of his order.

"Back in September, there was a pretty brutal murder," Detective Linebeck explained. "A woman named Whitney James was beaten to death in front of her apartment."

"Wait, I think I remember seeing that in the news a while ago," I said. "Something about a woman who was murdered a month ago and how they are still searching for the suspect."

"That's the one," Detective Linebeck said. "It blew up big and turned into a tabloid sideshow. The primary suspect is a man named Spencer Rhode. Our investigation revealed that Spencer had been stalking Whitney. Moreover, we collected DNA evidence that placed Spencer at the scene of the crime around the time of death."

Bennet placed his hands in his pockets, almost kicking his right leg in boredom. "Riveting…" he said in a dry, deadpan tone. "I'm gonna stab a guess that this is more than a simple one-and-done murder. They don't typically bring in a federal homicide detectives for a mundane crime of passion, and you'd never come crawling to ask for help with something so utterly banal."

Detective Linebeck dourly averted his gaze from Bennet. "We've been trying to keep it quiet, but since the murder of Whitney James, four more women have been killed," he said.

I gasped. "You mean to tell me that this guy has already killed five people in the span of roughly a month?" I asked in horror.

"At least," Detective Linebeck said darkly. "At the rate Spencer is going, someone else could be killed right now as we speak. There's no ruling out the possibility that other victims are yet to be discovered as well."

I might have been imagining it, but I couldn't shake the feeling of both shame and fear I sensed in Detective Linebeck's voice.

"Each victim was brutally beaten to death, and had some trace of evidence that linked Spencer to the scene of the crime. What's worse is that every victim so far also had blonde hair, just like Whitney's."

"So now you're dealing with a serial killer," Bennet said.

Detective Linebeck bit his lip. "Something much worse, actually," he said. "Every time a victim was killed, no one saw or heard it happen. Spencer's been declared missing since Whitney James's death, and we have a nationwide ABP set out for him, but no one's seen him or heard from him anywhere. We're running around like a bunch of chickens who got their heads cut off, scrambling to try and catch a perp made of smoke with our bare hands."

Despite everything I had seen involving Specters up until now, the idea that they were potentially involved in a series of brutal and violent crimes like this... Saying the thought was chilling would have been an understatement. A serial killer who disappears entirely after committing a murder sounded like something straight out of a slasher film.

"My duty is to protect and serve," Detective Linebeck said. "We've been keeping the details quiet to keep from starting a public panic, but I know with an investigation like this, we're in over our heads. If it means preventing countless deaths and saving lives, I'll swallow my pride as an investigator and go behind the backs of my superiors if I have to."

"Well, aren't you a standup guy?" Bennet scoffed. "I feel honored that you always trust me with such important things."

Detective Linebeck crossed his arms. "Trust is a strong word," he said. "Officially speaking, the man known as Bennet Grey doesn't exist, and I know about as little about you as I do about how Spencer Rhode has evaded arrest for as long as he has."

Bennet smirked. "Of course," he replied, "Bennet Grey is an assumed name, after all."

"Fair enough," Detective Linebeck said. "Every time I come to you, you get results. As long as you keep our arrangement private, I won't pry into your affairs. My gut's telling me it's better for everyone this way. Subdue Spencer Rhode, and I'll handle the rest."

"Business as usual then," Bennet said.

"That's everything, Bennet," Detective Linebeck said. "I'll be on my way now."

And with that, Detective Linebeck got back into his car. Bennet and I stepped out of the way as he pulled out and drove unceremoniously away. It was now our duty to track down a dangerous murderer and subdue him by any means necessary.

CHAPTER 11

A DISTURBING FAMILIARITY

"Ignite!" I shouted.

A fireball launched from my hand and torpedoed into a nearby training dummy. I continued to practice the spell in a patch of lawn behind Bennet's house in the Otherside.

A giant cherry blossom tree towered over Bennet's abode, dropping delicate pink flower petals like snow, some of which charred into ash before disappearing entirely as they got caught in the crossfire.

"Ignite!" I shouted once more, the fireball I launched making a loud banging sound upon hitting the training dummy.

"Well done," Bennett said, slowly clapping his hands, "I think you've earned a break."

Bennet sat sprawled out in a wicker armchair, holding a lit cigarette between his fingers, a small glass table with an ashtray on it set next to him.

I wiped the sweat off my brow before sitting down next to him in an adjacent chair.

"How are you feeling?" Bennet asked.

"I'm still trying to catch my breath, actually," I said with a light huff.

"It's only natural," he said. "Magic is the ability to make one's will a reality. At its apex, magic can even manifest a miracle. The bigger the spell, the more power it needs. It's only natural you'd be tired."

Bennet took a puff of his cigarette. "You've made a lot of progress in just a few days. When I first tried to cast that spell, I damn near singed my eyebrows off."

"Shouldn't we be chasing after that murderer Detective Linebeck told us about?" I asked.

Bennet ashed his cigarette. "Patience, Yuri," he said. "This isn't your run-of-the-mill killer or Specter here. We can't just rush in, guns blazing. Should it come down to it, I'm going to need you to be able to defend yourself."

His eyes narrowed, his expression suddenly somber as he took another puff. "I suspect the Specter involved is one called a Daemon Parasite," he said while exhaling smoke.

"What kind of Specter is that?" I asked.

Bennet put his cigarette out in the nearby ashtray. "They're nasty and cunning little bastards," he said. "They're weak and defenseless on their own, but they have a penchant for manipulating and possessing humans to compensate for it. They seek out vulnerable humans with some form of deep-seated resentment or insecurity and slowly erode their self-control. They whisper sweet nothings and temptations into the ears of their victims until they're completely powerless to resist their influence. Once the parasite fully takes hold, the victim's mind and soul slowly corrode away until they're empty husks the Parasite controls like a puppet."

I did everything I could to maintain a straight face, desperately trying not to think of the canary-shaped Specter that haunted my mother. I clenched my hands in my lap, staring out into the distance as I tried to separate myself from my uncomfortable feelings.

"A Daemon Parasite's MO is to force its victims into hurting others, feeding off the discord they sow," Bennet said. "As it steadily gains more control over its host, the human slowly becomes a berserker, far stronger than any normal person. Once someone's under the thrall of Daemon, it's only a matter of time before they are overtaken completely."

Bennet's eyes darkened. "Unless the Parasite is removed by a mage and exorcised, it'll eventually destroy their victim's soul," he said.

"It kills their victim, you mean?" I said.

"Worse, Yuri," he said. "Much, much worse."

A gentle breeze blew through the air.

"When a person dies, their soul returns to the Farside, where it awaits rebirth in the Sea of Souls," the mage explained. "However, if the soul is destroyed, that's the end of it. It can't return to the Farside. There is no rebirth, and there is no fixing what's been shattered beyond repair. Only oblivion awaits."

Bennet got up, stretching his arms. "Out of all the Specters I've encountered over the years, they're probably the type I hate the most. They're truly loathsome vermin."

Bennet's explanation left me in stunned silence.

Is this what happened to my mom? I thought to myself as a cold sweat dripped down the back of my neck. *Was my mother's soul destroyed by some monster attracted by a deep resentment she had for me? Was it because I lived and dad died that she—*

"Something wrong?" Bennet asked.

I snapped back into reality, quickly regaining my composure.

"It's nothing," I replied. "We can talk about it later. We should focus on Spencer."

"Alright...if you say so," he said, clearly hesitant to change the topic.

"Bennie!" a squeaky voice called.

At that moment, a pixie flew from the blades of grass below, fluttering around Bennet like an excitable dragonfly.

"Hello, Fornax," Bennet said. "It's been a while."

Fornax glanced my direction, their eyes glimmering with excitement.

"Oh, this one just heard!" Fornax exclaimed. "That human is Yuri-Birdie!"

"What kind of nickname is that?" I asked, both baffled and annoyed.

Fornax excitedly fluttered around us. "Pixies always struggle with human names, so these ones give new names to humans these ones are curious about," Fornax explained, giddy as they swarmed around my head. "This one heard about Yuri-Birdie from some pals over in the Observer's domain! No one's ever heard of Bennie taking on an apprentice before. Yuri-Birdie must be pretty special!"

I blushed with embarrassment. "I'm not special, though," I replied. "Really."

Bennet scoffed. "Don't let him fool you, Fornax," he said. "Yuri-Birdie, here is quite the talent."

Fornax landed on Bennet's shoulder.

"Something tells me you're not here this time just to play," Bennet said. "Is there something I can help you with?"

"Bennie is so smart!" Fornax exclaimed. "There's a big, scary, blobby mess nearby, and this one was hoping Bennie could make it go away."

"I'm on it, Fornax," Bennet said. "Which way is it?"

Fornax pointed towards the open field. "It's that way," they said. "It's a distance a mortal should be able to manage. Keep going straight, and Bennie can't miss it."

"Thank you, Fornax. Yuri-Birdie and I will take care of it right away," Bennet said.

I couldn't tell if he was genuinely amused by Fornax's nickname, or if he was simply screwing with me. He was like a little kid who kept on repeating the same joke for his own amusement.

"Be careful, Bennie!" Fornax said. "This one felt a scary presence there. It could still be hanging around."

"Thank you for the warning, Fornax," Bennet replied.

Fornax turned once again to address me. "This one wants to play with Yuri-Birdie sometime! So don't die out there! Okay?"

With that, Fornax waved goodbye and flew up into the boughs of the cherry blossom above.

"Fornax is one of my regulars," Bennet explained. "Unlike most pixies, Fornax's information is reliable. If we keep going that way, we're sure to find an Abscess and hopefully some lead on Spencer."

He flashed me a coy smile. "Ready to head out, Yuri-Birdie?" he asked.

I stood up, ignoring Bennet's shit-eating grin. "Lead the way, Bennie," I said.

#

Bennet and I trekked for about half a mile into the field behind his home. As we journeyed in the direction Fornax pointed us to, a faint odor started to fill the air. It wasn't long before Bennet and I spotted an odd tar-black lump off in the distance. It oozed like an infected boil rising from the land.

"The abscess is close," Bennet said. "Be careful."

"So this is what you meant about how Malevolence plagues the Otherside like a blight," I asked.

He nodded. "An Abscess is caused by an excess of Malevolence that congeals and putrefies in one area until it becomes like a cancerous growth to the Otherside. If left untreated, the corruption will spread and slowly start rotting away at the location's ability to sustain life," he said. "I said it once already, and I'll say it again: be careful."

The Abscess was stomach-churning and revolting up close. A black, sludge-like substance slowly ate away at the land below like a corrosive acid. Rising from the taint were inflamed red pustules that oozed the same sludge-like pus from a boil. The smell was like rotting meat. I could practically see the smoldering odor warping the space around the strange goo it emanated from. In the center were the remains of a giant four-legged beast, mangled and rotting away in the Malevolence that it rested in. The Poltergeists I'd encountered back in September felt like child's play compared to this cosmic horror decaying the Otherside before my eyes.

"So that's the Abscess... Isn't that a sight?" I dourly remarked, debating whether or not to pinch my nose.

"Yep," Bennet replied nonchalantly. "You'll get desensitized to the smell soon enough."

"What is that thing rotting in the middle there?" I asked, my stomach churning at the mere sight of it.

"Dunno," he replied. "It can wait, though. We need to cleanse the Malevolence here before we do anything else."

Bennet pointed towards a few of the nearby boils rising from the ground a few feet away. "Go over there and exorcise the Malevolence like you would a Specter," he instructed. "Those pustules are where the Malevolence has congealed the most. If we clear those out, the Abscess won't be able to sustain itself."

I gazed upon the black, tar-like substance and the pustules that looked like they could pop at any second, recoiling in instinctive disgust. "Is it even safe to be here?" I asked.

"Safe as it can be," Bennet sighed. "I don't sense any Specters hanging around, and even the strongest Others avoid an Abscess like the plague. Just don't go directly touching the pustules, and you'll be okay."

I pouted, annoyed. "Okay…" I grumbled, dreading the task ahead.

I reluctantly approached the group of pustules that Bennet instructed me to handle. They were even more sickening up close. It was like the black sludge was alive, and the red boil that putridly squatted on the land resembled a giant infected sore on someone's face. I closed my eyes and recalled my desire to protect other people from Specters.

"Blight and miasma that plagues this world," I called."I cleanse you of your despair. Begone from this reality."

The pustule writhed and screeched as it burst into a warm light. The sludge that pooled around scattered like dust in the wind as its source disappeared.

"Very good," Bennet cheered. "I'll handle the ones over there. Shout if anything comes up."

One by one, Bennet and I cleansed the Malevolence boils that formed this Abscess. As we made more progress, the pools of taint disappeared, and the stench of rotting meat steadily subsided with each area we purified. Even after we had cleared all the Malevolence, the grass beneath our feet remained dried and yellowed, like the area had gone through a prolonged drought.

"There," Bennet declared. "Now that the Abscess is cleansed, the land will be able to slowly heal itself."

"Do you think Spencer's the one who caused this?" I asked.

"Too soon to tell," Bennet replied. "Let's scour the area and see if we can find any clues about what started this."

I squirmed as I turned my attention to the mangled beast lying clear of the sludge that had been pooling over it.

"Ugh, I can't believe I'm even suggesting this," I groaned. "But let's start with that rotting animal corpse…thing. Nothing else is immediately out of place otherwise."

"Good idea," Bennet replied.

We moved in closer and inspected the mangled remains. The huge corpse almost resembled a giant lion. "Almost" was the primary operating word here, because it had another head sprouting out of its back that had been mostly stripped of its flesh, and a large black snake where its tail was supposed to be. The corpse's flesh had rotted to a point where I could make out exposed bone and sinew.

"What is that thing?" I moaned in disgust.

Bennet squatted next to the mangled set of remains.

"That's a chimera," he explained. "Among the denizens living here in the Otherside, a chimera is considered an apex predator of sorts. They're violent and very territorial."

Bennet gestured to the chimera's rotting second head and the snake it had for a tail.

"On top of having fearsome physical strength, it has the head of a goat with a penchant for uttering some nasty incantations, letting off curses, and other destructive spells. As if the physical assault and the magical onslaught weren't already deadly enough, it then throws in the snake head. The venom it administers with each bite could kill a human in less than a minute if it's not detoxed immediately."

Bennet squinted, surveying the corpse. "Still..." he thought aloud. "As violent as they are, chimeras aren't stupid enough to get caught in an Abscess, so if the Abscess didn't kill the chimera—bingo!"

"Did you find something?" I asked.

Bennet pointed to the beast's chest and stomach. It was covered in bruises and slashes, like a feral beast had beaten and clawed it into submission.

"Great, so there's something even worse out there that managed to kill this thing," I said with a shudder.

"I think it's very possible that this was Spencer's doing," Bennet said. "Remember what Linebeck said? About how his victims were all beaten to death?"

"There's no way a human could do that!" I retorted. "Just look at this thing! It'd snap a human in half like a toothpick!"

Bennet stood up, his expression grim.

"They could if they were fully possessed by a Daemon Parasite," he said darkly.

I looked upon the mangled corpse in horror, the sight only worsened by its torn sinew and the smell of decay. It was then that my nausea became too much to handle. Feeling my stomach jerk suddenly, I hunched over and vomited, almost falling to my knees. I took deep breaths, gagging and still reeling slightly as a cold sweat dripped from my forehead.

"You good?" Bennet asked.

"Sorry…" I weakly replied in between gags, focused on my breathing. "I'll be fine… Just give me a moment."

As I tried to catch my breath, I felt a pinch from behind my eyes as I looked upon the Chimera once more. I heard a voice whisper so quietly that I couldn't make out the words.

"Did you hear tha—" I said, before suddenly doubling over.

My head felt like it was being stabbed by a metal spike. The pain was blinding. I couldn't contain my screams as I doubled over.

"Please! Make it stop!" a voice screamed, *"Make it stop! I don't want to hurt anyone!"*

I couldn't make sense of what was going on around me. It was like all my senses were on fire as I was completely overwhelmed by the voice.

"Yuri!" Bennet called frantically.

I could barely make out the sound of Bennet's voice.

"I don't want this!" the voice screamed. *"Make it stop! Make it stop!"*

I fell to the ground, everything going dark.

CHAPTER 12

RESONANCE

I couldn't see anything. It felt like I was floating underwater. The feelings of someone else's fear and pain washed over me like a vicious ocean current. The sensation was so volatile, I was terrified that it would pull me under.

"I've never been good at anything," a man's voice echoed, mousy and quiet. *"I've never had anything I've been passionate about. I'm not rich, I don't have any useful skills, and I'm not even all that good-looking. I'm just an anonymous nobody destined to be forgotten by this world."*

I desperately tried to steady my breath.

"Despite all of that. The first time she smiled at me, I felt like I was somebody," the voice echoed.

An image formed in my mind. A man stood behind the cash register of a gas station convenience store. He was probably in his late twenties or early thirties, slim and homely, like he'd resigned himself into blending into the background for the rest of his life. He stood in the quiet store, looking so devoid of purpose that he would've bent under the force of whatever wind blew his way.

Every detail was somehow both distorted and crystal clear. It was like being stuck in that fuzzy in-between of dreaming and waking up.

The image shifted, and I saw the man sitting in a 50s-themed diner, in a booth by himself. A waitress came to take his order. She was tall, with rich and wavy blonde hair that she tied in a loose ponytail. A name tag reading "Whitney" was pinned to her shirt. I could hear the sound of a heart beating, the pulse steadily quickening as she approached the man.

"Hey, Spencer," Whitney greeted with a casual grin. "Take it you want your usual?"

Spencer gave a crooked, awkward smile. "Yes, please," he replied. "Thank you."

"You got it," she said playfully, writing the order down before walking away.

Spencer stared longingly as she moved on to her next table. *"She's the reason I come here so much,"* Spencer said, his voice echoing like he was narrating a scene in a movie.

He was entranced as he watched Whitney wipe down a few empty tables and take the orders of a few other customers. She made talking with other people look easy.

"It was love at first sight," Spencer's voice echoed. *"I was mesmerized by her smile, the way she moved… everything."*

Spencer looked away from Whitney and out the window he sat next to.

"It's stupid, though," his voice echoed. *"I'm stupid."*

A feeling of loneliness washed over me like a cold splash of water.

"She'd never go for a guy like me."

Was I witnessing Spencer's memories? Seeing the world as Spencer saw it? Bennet said I had a gift that was considered very rare, even among other mages. He called it Resonance. It had to be the cause of this weird dream-thing I was having. It felt strange watching Spencer go about his life. Was this timid man someone who would become a cold-blooded killer?

Spencer was lying in his bed. His bedroom was small, cramped, with a variety of trash and dirty clothes that littered the living space. The setting sun's warm glow peered through the cracks of the crooked blinds that hung in the bedroom window. Spencer scrolled through his phone, having found Whitney on several social media sites. He stared at a picture she'd posted where she'd wrapped her arms around the shoulders of two of her friends, beaming smiles on all their faces.

"I..." Spencer's voice echoed, trailing off.

The image that played out before my mind froze and distorted itself for a brief moment, like a glitch in video playback. When the image came back into focus, an eerie black spider the size of a baseball was perched on Spencer's shoulder by the nape of his neck. It had blood-red eyes and gave off a familiar aura of dread. There was no mistaking it: Spencer was haunted by a Specter.

"*I want to be a part of her life...*" Spencer's voice echoed darkly.

He once again sat in the diner where Whitney worked. He nervously tapped his finger against the table, blissfully unaware of the Specter that clung to him. Whitney came from the kitchen, carrying a plate loaded with a Reuben sandwich and French fries. She gently placed the plate in front of Spencer. I could feel his heart racing as he tried desperately to make eye contact with Whitney.

"Can I get you anything else?" she asked.

"Um," he stammered, his tongue tying into knots.

"*Come on! Say it!*" Spencer's voice echoed. "*Ask her out! Ask her out, you dumbass!*"

Spencer looked back down at his plate of food. "No, I'm okay," he said. "Thank you."

Whitney smiled before leaving to tend to another table. Spencer clenched his jaw in frustration.

"I'm such a coward..." his voice bitterly echoed.

The Specter's on Spencer's shoulder twitched and quivered.

"It's okay," the Specter cooed, gently and sweetly. "Even if you can't bring yourself to say your feelings out loud, that doesn't mean you can't pursue her, right?"

The light weakened in Spencer's eyes.

"Why let go of what your heart truly desires?" the Specter said.

A multitude of memories played out before my eyes. I watched as Spencer printed out pictures he found of Whitney online and hung them up on his bedroom walls. He stared longingly at a photo of her sitting in an armchair, slowly stroking his fingers down the image like he was in a trance. I could hear the sound of Spencer's heartbeat racing in excitement.

"I don't get it," Spencer's voice echoed. *"I chickened out... It should have been over."*

More memories played before my eyes. Events that all took place over four weeks blazed into my mind like the flash of a camera. I watched as Spencer followed Whitney home from work and stared at the window of her apartment building from his car down below. I watched Spencer as he followed Whitney on her days off, taking pictures from a distance as she shopped at the mall or market. When Whitney went to see a movie with a friend, he sat in the back row of the theatre watching her like she was the movie.   A feeling of unease washed over me like the trickle of ice-cold water slowly dripping down my arm.

"But why?" Spencer's voice cried. *"Why can't I get Whitney out of my head?"*

Spencer sat in his car parked down the street below Whitney's apartment once more, gazing upon her window like a wolf would stare down a full moon. His eyes were hollow. There was no light in them. They were cold, almost like that of a cockroach. The Specter sat upon his shoulder like a spider sitting atop a throne. Whitney emerged from the building wearing sweats and carrying a trash bag. Spencer's eyes were fixed upon her as she carried the bag to a dumpster out in the parking lot.

"Now's the time," the Specter said. "Lay your heart bare."

Spencer got out of his car. Whitney tossed the trash bag into the dumpster. As she turned around to return to her apartment, she jumped at Spencer's sudden appearance.

"Whitney," he greeted.

She stood there, apprehensive, her shoulders stiff as she nervously bit her lip. "Who are you?" she asked.

Spencer stepped closer, his eyes and smile manic. "You remember me, don't you?" he asked.

Whitney shuddered, taking a step back from Spencer. "Should I?" she replied, trying to steady her trembling voice.

"I mean, it was love at first sight for me," Spencer chimed. "Since the first day I met you, I couldn't stop thinking about you."

Whitney froze as Spencer continued to rant.

"I've been following you wherever you go!" he exclaimed. "I want to know everything about you! I want to be a part of your life!"

"You..." Whitney said coldly. "You're that guy from the diner. Spencer."

Her fearful gaze transformed into a furious glare.

"You've been following me? What the fuck is wrong with you?" she shouted. "Get the hell away from me, you creeper!"

Time came to a grinding halt. Spencer's excitement was replaced with stone silence in the face of Whitney's outburst. The scene in my mind paused for a moment, leaving her mid-yell, mouth agape.

"It wasn't supposed to be like this," Spencer's voice echoed.

The Specter on his shoulder quivered. "What a shame," It said. "This mouthy girl doesn't understand how lucky she is to have your love."

The light left Spencer's eyes completely. He slowly crept closer to Whitney.

"This girl needs to be put in her place," the Specter said.

Spencer stroked her cheek, his hand gentle and serene as he was entranced by the Specter's voice. He exhaled, the sound of his breath almost booming in the silent void the Specter had created.

"Go ahead," the Specter urged. "You don't have to hold back anymore. Destroy everything you despise to your heart's content."

Gritting and baring his teeth like a feral animal, Spencer snarled as he tackled Whitney to the ground. His anger washed over my body like scalding water. I wanted to scream, but all I could do was watch as Spencer punched, slashed, and clawed at Whitney like a deranged beast. After one final, brutal punch that made a violent cracking sound, Spencer stood up, taking deep, heavy breaths as he surveyed what remained of Whitney on the ground, bloodied and barely recognizable. I could smell the iron from the blood that soaked his hands.

The light returned to Spencer's eyes. He stared in horror at Whitney's corpse before slowly fixing his gaze to the carnage that soaked his shaking hands.

"What did I just do?" He trembled. "Why did I do this? I didn't want this!"

Spencer fell to his knees.

"Whitney!" he screamed.

The Specter crawled up to the nape of his neck as he started sobbing. "Don't be sad," it said. "Didn't it feel good to finally let loose all that pent-up rage? This world is awful. There's no need to hold yourself back anymore. Unleash the fury deep within you and destroy everything about this world you despise."

The Specter sank its spider fangs deep within Spencer's neck. The light fully left his eyes once more as he stood up.

"This world..." he said coldly. "...is shit!"

He spat on Whitney's corpse.

"She was supposed to be a nice girl, but she rejected me!" Spencer exclaimed, flashing a deranged grin. "She didn't deserve me, and I did the world a service getting rid of a bitch like her!"

He cackled. "Good riddance, I say!"

My body burned like I was being bathed in boiling water. I screamed in silence, Spencer's thoughts echoing and screeching all around me.

"I loved her!"

"Why did I hurt her?"

"Whitney, I'm sorry!"

It felt like I was being pulled apart from the inside out, as I watched more memories flash before my eyes. One by one, I watched as Spencer brutally maimed woman after woman like a feral beast. Their screams rang in my ears. I watched as Spencer brutally butchered the dead chimera from before, moving and swiping wildly like a demon straight out of Hell.

"Please! Make it stop!" Spencer's voice cried. *"Make it stop! Make it stop! I don't want to hurt anyone! Make it stop!"*

A new and familiar voice pierced through the maelstrom of pain in which I swirled.

"Yur…" it whispered weakly, "Wa…up.."

The voice was soft, and I could barely make it out.

"Yur…plea…wake up…" it called again.

The voice became clearer. I pictured it like a spider's thread being spun into the depths of the underworld. I imagined myself reaching out my right hand and grasping it as tightly as I could.

"Yuri! Please wake up!"

CHAPTER 13

THE KILLER HAUNTED

BY A DAEMON PARASITE

When I opened my eyes, I was lying in Bennet's arms. His face was pale as a ghost as his frightened eyes met my gaze, the ends of his red bangs tickling my nose slightly.

"Yuri!" he called.

The fear in his voice felt off-putting and surreal; it was so uncharacteristic of him. That fear chilled me to my bones. I felt sluggish, like I had woken up from a nightmare. My hands and face felt cold, and my mouth was dry.

"What happened?" I asked, still slightly dazed.

"Out of nowhere, you just started screaming!" Bennet exclaimed. "The next thing I know, you're on the ground, writhing in pain."

I sat up, slowly regaining my senses. I clutched my forehead, recalling the visions I saw.

"You were right, Bennet," I said. "Spencer was the one to kill this chimera. I saw it."

"So when you passed out, you saw Spencer killing the chimera?"

"No," I said weakly.

Bennet helped me off the ground.

"I didn't just see him kill the chimera," I said. "I saw him fall in love with Whitney. I saw him get possessed by the Demon Parasite and start stalking her."

I felt my body shaking as I recalled everything I saw and felt.

"I watched him brutally beat Whitney to death and do the same thing to any other woman who remotely resembled her. I felt his pain and guilt. I kept on hearing his voice scream out that he didn't want any of this to happen, begging for someone, anyone, to make it stop."

Bennet sighed. "That's Resonance at work again," he said. "I never experienced it firsthand, but my teacher said it was easy to feel completely overwhelmed when bonding with someone else's soul the way you just did. You feel their emotions and experience the world as they did. If Spencer's turmoil was that volatile, it's little wonder you passed from it."

I took a deep breath, still rattled from the waking nightmare on steroids I'd just experienced. It was already a lot to take in on its own, but the Specter that haunted him—the way it spoke and coaxed Spencer into letting go of his inhibitions—it reminded me of the creature that haunted my mom.

Was this why my mom died? Was her soul truly gone for good?

Those thoughts raced through my mind in a rush of anxiety and panic. I clapped my hands to my face. I didn't have the luxury of worrying about that, not while Spencer remained at large.

"Well, cause of your Resonance misadventure, we know Spencer was here at some point," Bennet said. "If only we knew where he went after that."

I closed my eyes. "It's strange," I said. "It's like I can still feel him nearby. It's weak, almost like a whisper, but I can hear his heart crying out."

I took a slow breath in and then slowly exhaled, clearing my mind. I focused on the grass that crunched under my feet and the delicate breeze that caressed my ears. As I strained my ears, I could hear a whisper off in the distance. I opened my eyes.

"There," I said. "Spencer's somewhere in that direction."

"Over in that direction is a place Others call the Forsaken Woods," Bennet explained. "It used to be home to some elves, but it was decimated by an Abscess a long time ago. Even after it was cleansed, the Abscess destroyed that area's ability to sustain life. Plants don't grow, and there isn't a single breeze to be felt. Over time, any living creature that remains there will still start to rot from the inside. Nothing short of a Specter could hope to survive in that hellscape long-term."

I gazed off in the direction of the Foresaken Woods.

"We should get moving," I said. "We have to stop Spencer before he hurts anyone else and before the Demon Parasite destroys his soul."

Bennet nodded.

"Lead the way, Yuri," Bennet said.

#

I lead Bennet through the winding fields of the Otherside. As we continued onward, I could start to sense the despair that flooded Spencer's heart, as if it were a gut instinct.

There was no telling what would await us when we finally managed to track down Spencer. Based on my vision, he was violent and unpredictable. He'd probably attack us, and would be unable to stop himself unless we separated him from the Demon Parasite that sunk its fangs into his neck.

The closer we got to Spencer's presence, the more the grass beneath our feet wilted and withered. The terrain eventually gave way to a sickly grey dirt that shifted loosely like sand in a barren desert. The sky slowly turned to a dull and sickly sepia-toned yellow. Off in the distance, I could make out a bundle of black trees without any leaves.

"Spencer's in there," I said. "I'm sure of it."

Bennet scanned the horizon. "Looks like he and that Parasite did end up setting up shop in the Forsaken Woods," he said. "If the Parasite whisked him away to the Otherside every time he killed someone, it would explain why he's been able to avoid getting caught for so long."

This part of the Otherside felt wrong. A sense of unease filled the air, making it feel stagnant and stale. It was like the area was frozen in time by sadness, and the fabric of reality in this place was slowly rotting away.

"Even those possessed by a Demon Parasite can only last out for so long before their body starts to mutate from the corruption here," Bennet said. "We need to keep going."

We journeyed on, reaching the forest's edge. The trees towered over us, but each one was shriveled and leafless. Dead soil crunched beneath our feet. The quiet of the Forsaken Woods was just as ominous as it was melancholy. The whole area was the embodiment of the word "lifeless."

"Spencer's deep inside," I said. "But it's weird; I can't pin down where now."

I strained my ears and mind, desperate for any sign of our target. All I could hear were faint, incoherent whispers that had no clear origin.

"It's almost like his feelings are holding their breath," I said.

Bennet scoured the boughs of the trees above. "Fitting spot for a Demon Parasite," he mused.

Bennet briefly stared into the distance, his expression somber, before he spoke. "Yuri, I want you to be prepared if we have to kill Spencer," he said. "He's certain to attack us, and there's a good chance we might need to put him out of his misery here and now."

I flinched. After experiencing Spencer's pain firsthand, the idea of killing him felt unthinkable.

"Will it come to that?" I asked.

"Only one way to find out," Bennet replied darkly. "Come on, and stay close."

I nodded, unable to voice a response.

The deeper we went into the Forsaken Woods, the more unnerving it became. No sunshine drifted through the boughs above. The air was completely still. Not a single living creature could be seen or heard as far as the eye could see. A desolate sorrow dwarfed us like the towering, rotted trees that surrounded the area. Even without the possibility of Spencer jumping out and attacking us, these decaying remains of a forest creeped me out.

"Can you sense Spencer at all?" Bennet asked.

I scanned the area. "Yes and no," I said. "It's like something's hiding his presence."

The fog thickened. I could barely see a few feet in front of me.

"This fog is weird," I thought aloud. "Is this normal here?"

There was no response.

"Bennet?" I called.

I scrambled, turning in various directions, desperate for any sign of him.

"Bennet!" I called again. "Where are you?"

The fog was too thick, and I couldn't see Bennet anywhere. I was all alone, the eerie quiet of the Forsaken Woods only emphasizing that awful fact. I pulled the charm from my pocket, holding it by the string. It flickered like a dying light bulb.

"Yuri...whe...you?" Bennet's voice called weekly through the stone,

The charm's meager light faded entirely. I slowly returned the charm to my pocket, hands trembling, my heart racing. I breathed as silently as I possibly could, terrified that even the slightest sound could attract certain doom. I quietly and frantically surveyed my surroundings, desperately trying to find some sign of Bennet.

"Damn it, Bennet... where are you?" I whispered to myself.

I saw a shadow off in the distance. It slowly grew larger as it approached. I remained completely still, desperately praying that it was Bennet.

"Kill... Rip... Tear..." a voice echoed in the distance.

The voice sounded gargled and distorted. I held my breath, fearing I already knew who it belonged to.

"Kill... Smash... Gut..." the shadow said.

It crept closer.

"Kill... Rip... Smash... Tear... Kill..."

Spencer Rhode emerged from the fog. His skin was greyed, like his flesh was decomposing. Black sludge oozed from behind his eyes and dripped out from his nose, ears, and mouth. The Demon Parasite that had styled itself after a spider was now fused to Spencer's neck, swollen like a tumor. His fingers were outstretched like claws, and he shuffled like a zombie.

"Kill… Rip… Tear… Kill!" Spencer roared.

I stared in frozen horror as he staggered and slunk his way closer. The growth on his neck, where the Demon Parasite had fused to him, twitched and pulsated.

"Kill the boy," the parasite hissed. "He and his companion seek to end us both."

"Kill… Rip…. Tear…" Spencer growled.

I retreated slowly, trembling. Spencer pounced at me like a feral animal, swiping his hands wildly.

"Kill!" he roared.

I leaped backward, falling down and narrowly avoiding Spencer's swiping claws. I quickly scrambled back to my feet, raising my trembling right hand and holding it steady with my left.

"Ignite!" I shouted.

A fireball launched from my hand and torpedoed at Spencer. The projectile made a direct hit against his chest, exploding on impact. When the smoke and embers cleared, Spencer continued creeping closer without even a scratch.

"Ignite!" I shouted over and over again, launching a multitude of fiery orbs at Spencer.

It was no use; he shrugged each one off. It was like I was throwing ping-pong balls at an undead knight in plate armor.

"Hurry up and kill him, you fool!" the Parasite screeched.

"Kill…" Spencer growled.

My eyes darted between the ground and the nearby trees. I raised my right hand again, aiming at the trees closest to Spencer.

"Ignite!" I shouted again.

I launched several fireballs at those trees, instantly setting them ablaze. The flames spread easily to their dried, barren neighbors. Spencer screeched, thrashing and flailing his arms as the fire consumed him. Now was my chance. I bolted, running away with all the speed I could muster.

"Ignite!" I called.

I launched more fireballs at the trees I passed, setting them ablaze in a desperate attempt to slow down Spencer.

"Bennet! Where the hell are you!" I shouted angrily as I continued to run.

Bennet was nowhere to be seen. I continued to sprint, my chest on fire as I struggled to get enough air into my lungs. Before I realized it, I fell, tripping over a rogue tree root. When I came to my senses, Spencer loomed above me, ready to kill.

"Die…" he growled in a deep guttural whisper.

I was desperate. I didn't want to die. Not now.

"Please, Spencer!" I said. "Please don't do this! I know you don't want to hurt anyone!"

Spencer twitched erratically like a broken toy. "Make it stop…" he muttered.

"This isn't what you wanted, Spencer!" I said. "I saw the horror in your eyes when Whitney died! You would never in your right mind want to kill someone!"

Fresh black sludge rolled down from behind his eyes and down his cheeks like tears. "I…don't want this…" he whimpered. "Make…it stop… Make it stop!"

"You fool!" the Parasite boomed.

The growth on Spencer's neck twitched violently. Spencer writhed in pain, the sound of his snapping bones echoing off into the distance.

"You dare defy me!" the Parasite roared.

Spencer reared towards me, readying again to kill.

"That's enough!" Bennet called.

Rings of light appeared around Spencer, binding his arms and legs and causing him to fall forward on the ground. He struggled, flailing violently in a futile effort to free himself. The Demon Parasite leaped off Spencer's neck, a small stream of black sludge pouring out from where it had latched itself. It quickly tried to scuttle away, but in a quick, fluid motion, Bennet crushed it under his foot. He ground it under his heel with a sickening crunch.

"Foul Specter that blights this world," Bennet said coldly. "I cleanse you of your despair. Begone from this reality."

Bennet's words were cold and sharp like a knife as he practically ordered the Parasite out of existence. It screeched, bursting into a bright light from under Bennet's loafer.

"Good riddance…" he spat. Bennet cracked his neck before turning his attention to me. "You did a good job holding out as long as you did. Are you hurt?"

"I'm fine," I replied.

"Good. That's one less headache to deal with later."

Bennet took a sullen deep breath, now directing his focus to Spencer. "Yuri, please look away," he said. "I don't want you to see what I'm about to do."

"You don't mean…" I stammered. "The Parasite is gone! Spencer didn't want any of this to happen! The Parasite drove him to do this! We have to save him! We *have to*."

"His soul is beyond saving, Yuri," Bennet replied. "Because of the Specter's influence, his soul shattered into pieces, and his body is practically falling apart from long-term exposure to the corruption here. Don't forget he murdered five people. Regardless of his intentions and what caused it, those innocent women are dead because of him. There's nothing else that can be done for him now."

My eyes widened. "But I… This can't be—"

"Do you think I take pleasure in this? I hate that I have to do this, too!" Bennet snapped.

My words failed me. I stood before Bennet, stunned by his sudden outburst.

Bennet sheepishly looked away, trying to pull himself together. "I'm sorry, I shouldn't have lost my cool like that," he said.

Spencer thrashed weakly on the ground. "Make it stop… I don't want to hurt anyone…" he muttered weakly.

Bennet's expression was as mournful as it was grim. He looked upon Spencer as if he were a wounded deer.

"The only thing we can do now, Yuri, is to put him out of his misery," Bennet said. "I'm sorry. I'll make sure he isn't in pain for long."

It broke my heart. Despite the things Spencer had done under the Parasite's power, he was still a victim here. But as much as I wanted to deny it, there was nothing we could do for Spencer. He was beyond saving, and there was nothing anyone could do about it.

"Please…" Bennet pleaded quietly. "Look away now."

I bit my lip, struggling with the bitter taste once again induced by powerlessness.

"Okay," I said begrudgingly.

I turned my back on Spencer and Bennet, bracing myself for what was going to happen next.

"Ignite!" Bennet called.

I felt a blast of heat from behind and saw the warm red glow of fire against the decaying trees in front of me. Spencer screamed for less than a second before going completely silent. The sound reverberated in my ears and brain over and over again as the embers burned. When the flames finally dispersed…

Not even ash remained.

CHAPTER 14

CLOSURE

It had been a few days since Bennet and I had completed Detective Linebeck's request. We sat silently on our usual couches in Bennet's cottage. It was the first time we'd met up since returning from the Forsaken Forest. I was tired and still a little shellshocked from everything that happened. Now and then, my mind wandered off, and I could still hear the sound of Spencer's screams in the back of my brain. Bennet had reached out and asked me to meet him in the Otherside to discuss the case.

"So that's that," he said, finally breaking the silence. "I informed Detective Linebeck that Spencer won't be able to hurt anyone anymore. He was suspicious, but he didn't pry for any details. He's already handling everything on his side so that the investigation will be closed without issue."

"That's good," I muttered half-heartedly.

Nothing about what had happened felt right. It was all so messed up and unfair. Spencer's insecurities attracted a Demon Parasite, and the Specter took advantage of his crush on Whitney and drove him to kill her and four other women. When everything was said and done, the tragedy ended with the deaths of six people.

"I get it: that whole affair left a sour taste in the mouth," Bennet said. "The outcome wasn't exactly a resounding success."

I sulked, not even responding. Bennet stood up and sat down next to me.

"I wish I could say this doesn't happen a lot, Yuri," Bennet said. "But a lot of my requests tend to go by the wayside and end badly. People or Others end up getting hurt, and a lot of the time, a job just ends in a bunch of loose ends and with zero closure. I know it's not fair, but that's life. We're here one moment and gone the next. Things may wrap up nicely in fiction, but in real life, it's very rare for someone to get a clean, happy ending."

I looked up at Bennet. "How do you deal with it then?" I asked.

Bennet gave me a melancholy smile. "I take the small wins where I can," he said. "Spencer can't hurt anyone anymore, and I know we saved a lot of lives by stopping him. This request ended far from ideally, but life is too precious a thing to spend its entirety fixating on everything that went wrong. All we can do is pick ourselves up whenever we fall and keep moving forward."

"You're right, Bennet," I replied, "I still just need some time to process everything, I guess."

"Take all the time you need, Yuri," he said. "You saw Spencer's memories and feelings firsthand. The way my teacher described what Resonance felt like... I can barely imagine how nightmarish all of this was for you."

That's right; Bennet's teacher also possessed Resonance. I thought to myself.

"Can you tell me about your teacher, Bennet?" I asked. "You mentioned him several times now, but I still don't know anything about him. What was he like?"

Bennet groaned. "I figured you'd ask sooner or later," he grumbled. "Let me grab a cigarette. It's a long story."

Bennet rummaged through a nearby cabinet and returned with a pack of cigarettes and sat across from me like usual. He lit the cigarette with a blue flame conjured from the tip of his thumb and took a puff before he spoke.

"My teacher was an incredible mage," he said, exhaling smoke. "Even among the most prestigious of magi, Resonance was an incredibly rare gift. It is probably because of that gift that he developed a deep love for both people and Others. He seemed to have had a natural affinity for all living things, and wished to learn all there was about Others and the very fabric of our reality. In doing so, he came to understand the true nature of the Malevolence Phenomenon and the Specters whom mages had spent countless years fighting and exorcising. From that point on, my teacher devoted himself to studying Specters, the Malevolence Phenomena, and the Otherside, believing it to be in the best interest of everyone to cleanse and study the blight that plagued both the Nearside and the Otherside. In the end, he concluded that the best way for him to continue preserving the balance of reality was to bind himself to the Otherside."

"What do you mean?" I asked.

"Others live far longer than humans," Bennet said. "My teacher developed a workaround of sorts so he could live alongside them."

Bennet took another puff of his cigarette, ashing it in a nearby ashtray before he continued.

"My teacher discarded his original name and gave up his place in history to bind his soul to the Otherside, essentially freezing his body in time," he wearily explained. "The apex of magic is the ability to manifest a miracle. However, to manifest a miracle of that scale, something of equal value must be offered up in exchange. The price for his selective immorality was his legacy."

Bennet leaned back, resting his legs on the coffee table. "And that's all I can tell you about him," he said.

"Are you not allowed to talk about him or something?" I asked

Bennet shook his head. "That's all I remember."

I didn't understand. Bennet's teacher sounded like he was important to him, so how could his memory have failed him beyond general details?

"You can't be serious," I said.

"Dead serious," Bennet replied.

He took another puff of his cigarette.

"That was the price paid for his miracle," Bennet said, exhaling smoke once more. "To be unknown in life and unknown in death. When he first discarded his name and bound his soul to the Otherside, everyone he had ever known up until then forgot he had ever existed. When he named his successor and released his soul to return it to the Farside, everyone he met during his 'second life' came to forget him as well. It was like he never existed at all."

There was a slight bitterness to Bennet's words.

"That man meant the world to me, and I can't even remember his name or tell you what he looked like. The only people who do remember him are the Observer and the Collector, and they're strictly forbidden from ever revealing any personal details about him."

I sat dumbfounded and saddened by what he had said, still wrapping my head around Bennet's explanation.

"That's terrible…" I thought aloud. "I couldn't imagine what it would be like to just be completely erased from history and doomed to remain anonymous for the rest of eternity."

Bennet sullenly rested his head on the arm of the couch, placing his free hand over his eyes.

"It was a steep price to pay, but my teacher saw his mission as something worth sacrificing his entire legacy for," he said. "Pity it only delayed the inevitable. Even if one's body is undying, a soul can only last for so long before it must return to the Farside. It wasn't like he could linger in this world forever. Something tells me he knew all of this and went through with it anyway. I wouldn't be surprised if he were the sentimental type who was satisfied with the arrangement as long as there was someone who could carry the mantle once it was his turn to pass it on to someone else. That's probably why he went out of his way to name me his successor."

I recalled something from when we met Detective Linebeck to take his request. He'd mentioned that the man known as Bennet Grey didn't officially exist, and Bennet even clarified that the name he was using was an alias. I always wondered why Bennet had this otherworldly knowledge and how he sometimes spoke like he wasn't even born in this century. Was this why?

"Did you do it?" I asked. "Bind your soul to the Otherside, I mean. Will I forget you someday?"

Bennet flinched at my question before looking away in shame.

"Not quite, I'm afraid..." he said glumly. "My circumstances are a little different."

I had never seen Bennet act like this until now. The sadness in his voice as he looked away from me made it feel like he was deeply ashamed of something. He quickly composed himself once more, sitting back up and putting on his usual laid-back devil-may-care grin.

"That's enough depressing talk," he said. "Besides, you have finals coming up. Don't neglect your studies. After everything that's happened, you've earned some time off. We can resume your training after the holidays."

"Okay," I replied.

#

I got up and left, bidding Bennet farewell before I returned to my apartment. So many thoughts raced through my mind.

Bennet's teacher had sacrificed his legacy for something he believed in, choosing to contribute to the world even if it meant fading into obscurity, and that sacrifice only delayed his inevitable demise.

Amy struggled with her feelings of loneliness and isolation, and it attracted a Poltergeist that almost killed her multiple times.

Spencer couldn't bring himself to vocalize his affection for Whitney out loud, and in the end, both of them and four other women died because of the Demon Parasite that drove Spencer insane.

Meanwhile, I almost died long before I could even remember the near-death experience, and it left me with a curse that made my life feel like a living hell.

And then there was Mom…

Did we live only to suffer? Was this the universe's idea of some sick joke? Those questions were mysteries I would never know the answer to. What I did know, even after everything that I had witnessed and learned, was that I wasn't ready to give up on life just yet—as masochistic and foolish as it was.

The Demon Parasite… I was certain that was the type of Specter that had haunted Mom. I wanted to know why she died the way she did, and if there was something I could have done to save her. I didn't want to torture myself over the hypotheticals and what-ifs anymore. Even if it hurt me, I wanted to live my life without doubt and die without regret.

That was my wish, and the miracle I'd make my reality.

CHAPTER 15

THE QUESTIONS

LEFT UNANSWERED

I stood on a rooftop, the sky a creamy orange like the color of marmalade from the setting sun. A gentle breeze blew against my face.

How many times had I stood upon this rooftop now? How many times had I revisited this memory? How many times had I revisited this pain, this sorrow? I cannot recall.

I watched in horror as my mom stood on the rooftop's ledge with an eerie, otherworldly canary perched on her shoulder.

"Mom!" I screamed.

My mother turned her head back to look at me, a weak and tender smile on her face.

"Yuri...I'm sorry I couldn't be a better mother to you..." she said.

She then closed her eyes and stepped off the ledge. I fell to my knees as everything went utterly silent. In that moment, my entire world shattered before my eyes. In my state of shock and sheer devastation, I couldn't even hear the sound of my own screaming.

#

I opened my eyes, yet again groggy and tired from a poor night's sleep caused by this recurring dream. The date was December 21st. I'd managed to finish my classes and score high marks on my final exams despite everything weighing on my mind as of late. I was on winter break now.

Amy had already wished me goodbye and a "Happy Holidays!" before returning home to upstate New York to spend Christmas with her family. I chose to stay here like I did last year. My extended family hated having me around, and the feeling had become quite mutual. Spending Christmas alone in a quiet apartment felt far more preferable.

I rolled to my side, watching as snow gently fell outside my window. When it became clear that I wouldn't be able to fall back asleep, I begrudgingly sat up and got out of bed. I made sure to grab a black leather book that was placed on a folding table next to my bed. I placed it down on my counter while preparing some instant coffee before sitting back down to read it.

The book was old, with handwritten text neatly marked down in charcoal black ink.

#

...the Demon Parasite is a truly vile specimen. This Specter poses little threat to others on its own, but what it lacks in strength, it more than makes up for in cunning. Where most Specters function on pure instinct and attraction to despair, the Demon Parasite is calculating and manipulative in its approach. When it finds a vulnerable human, it latches onto them and whispers sweet nothings into the ears of its host to bolster itself and entice them, slowly driving their victims to inflict gruesome violence and atrocities upon others. Even if the Demon Parasite's prey cannot feel its presence, they are powerless to resist the bidding of the Parasite as it overrides their desires. They'll become mindless, physically enhanced berserkers whom the Demon Parasite uses as a puppet—

#

The text went on while also featuring some hand-drawn diagrams and illustrations of various Demon Parasites, information that I already knew well after reading through this journal three times already. I'd practically memorized its contents.

Bennet had a great deal of these journals stored away in the Otherside. They all contained various notes and observations regarding Specters, the Otherside, Others, and the Malevolence Phenomenon. These weighty tomes were the only things that remained of Bennet's former teacher, and even then, they still weren't much of a legacy. Any information that would have pertained to the personal details or opinions of the man who wrote them was wiped from the pages like the ink had been stripped away with bleach. These journals contained nothing about their original writer beyond their expertise. Bennet was more than kind enough to lend me a few of these tomes at a time, and I'd been scouring through them and researching almost every waking moment I could since the semester ended..

I wanted to know what happened to my mom four years ago. I'd started out researching Daemon Parasites, comparing my memories to the ones I'd experienced from Spencer via Resonance, and referencing the information I had gleaned from the borrowed journal. Between what I learned from these various records and the similarities between Spencer's haunting and my mom's, I had all but fully confirmed that the Specter that haunted her was a Daemon Parasite.

However, there was one clear difference between Spencer's textbook case of Daemon Parasite possession and what happened to my mother four years ago. These Specters always drove their victims to attack others, and every action it took was a means of survival. The Specter that haunted Mom, on the other hand, had constantly coaxed her to kill me, but when the dust settled, I survived, and the life that Mom took was her own.

That was the crucial component in this puzzle that I couldn't figure out for the life of me. Why did Mom die the way she did? The mystery I pursued was as confusing as it was emotionally painful. I moaned in restless frustration, closing my eyes and massaging my temples in an attempt to ease the logical conundrum that buzzed in my brain like a hornet's nest. It felt like I was running in circles and fumbling in the dark. I was lost and afraid, and I knew deep down that the true circumstances that surrounded Mom's death could turn out to be even worse than I thought. Even knowing all that, I couldn't bring myself to give up on my quest for answers. Whether you wanted to call it curiosity, self-torment, or a need for closure, I had to know the truth, no matter how awful it could have been.

I entered Bennet's home in the Otherside after I finished my coffee and washed up for the day. I carried a stack of large, leather-bound journals under one of my arms and brought them to the sitting room, where Bennet was lying down on a couch and reading an Agatha Christie novel I had lent him. He read the book intently, not even addressing my presence as I returned the journals I had borrowed to the bookshelves they called home, before grabbing a few new ones to bring with me back to my apartment. Just as I was about to leave, Bennet spoke up.

"Burning the candle from both ends of the wick, are we?" he asked without lifting his gaze from the book.

"There's some more stuff I want to learn about," I replied, trying not to elaborate on the specifics.

He folded the corner of his current page and closed the book, placing it on the coffee table in front of him.

"I've been keeping track of the journals you've been borrowing, you know," he said. "You barely say a word every time you come by to grab more, yet you seem awfully interested in any journal containing information about Daemon Parasites."

I glared at him. "What of it?" I replied.

"Do I have to spell it out for you? Something's been troubling you since our last request."

Bennet crossed his arms, his eyes stern like a parent getting ready to lecture their child.

"So let's stop beating around the bush," he declared. "What's going on? Out with it."

I should have known better than to think I could've kept a secret like that from Bennet for long. It would have been better to talk to him right then and there, because he wouldn't drop the subject otherwise. I set my latest stack of journals neatly on the coffee table before I sat on the couch opposite Bennet.

"Do you remember when you told my fortune when we first met?" I asked. "The part about how my mom died four years ago?"

"Yes," Bennet replied.

I nodded. When I spoke, it was with a sad weariness. I had let myself become numb to this pain, primarily for the sake of survival. Despite that, it was an emotional burden that still haunted me, even though I could fake a smile through it by now. My recurring nightmares of that day were a testament to that fact.

"My mom was haunted by a Specter. I'm pretty sure, in some way, it drove her to suicide," I said. "I wasn't able to put the pieces together until recently, but I'm positive that Specter was a Daemon Parasite. I constantly heard it trying to goad her into killing me because I was a burden she was better off without. Because of that, I believed it was my fault somehow that my mom chose to do what she did. I still do—a little part of me, at least, I mean."

Bennet sat and listened to my story, the sad concern quite plain on his face as I continued to speak.

"But something's been bothering me about it lately," I explained. "The more I read up on Daemon Parasites and other Specters, the idea of a Daemon Parasite driving my mom to take her own life sounds more and more unlikely. Daemon Parasites almost exclusively drive their victims to inflict harm on others. If that's the case, why was she the one to die?"

I sighed, once again resisting the urge to just surrender to the sadness of it all.

"I just wanna figure out what happened. I wanna know if it was my fault or not. I don't like not knowing anymore," I said.

"I'm sorry that I didn't say anything to you about it before. Truth be told, I'm so used to handling everything on my own that it didn't even occur to me to bring it up to you or ask for your thoughts."

I felt sharp tension in my chest after I shared my past and feelings with Bennet. I wasn't sure how he would react. Was he going to scold me? Lecture me? Go on and on about the importance of opening up to others? Tell me I screwed up with my research and say that my mom was haunted by another type of Specter that I never even heard of? I had no idea.

Finally, almost like he was reluctant to do so, Bennet replied to me.

"I think I know how we can figure out how your mom died," he said.

CHAPTER 16

A SURPRISING OPPORTUNITY

I stared in stunned disbelief, floored by Bennet's words.

"What did you say?" I asked, unsure whether I'd even heard him correctly.

"I know how we can figure out what happened to your mom, Yuri," he replied.

"How?" I asked, fighting the urge to stand up.

Bennet groaned, practically sulking in frustration. "Ugh, I can't believe I'm suggesting this..." he muttered to himself.

"Would you come out and say it already!" I demanded, starting to lose my patience.

He shifted uncomfortably in his seat, practically glaring in disgust at whatever he was about to suggest. "Do you remember that Other who gave you that cryptic warning a little after we first met?"

I instantly recalled the Other known as Peter, who called himself the Collector, and the cryptic warning he'd given me to stay away from Bennet. So much had happened since September that I'd barely even thought about him, or his warning, until Bennet mentioned it just now.

"Why him?" I asked. "Why would he know?"

Bennet sighed. "I mentioned his role before, haven't I?" he said. "The Observer, Lucia, records the names of people and others who are born, cataloging their lives from birth to death. Her counterpart, Peter, also known as the Collector, does the opposite. He records the names of those who die and the circumstances of their death before guiding their souls back to the Farside, watching over and protecting them as they await rebirth."

Bennet scowled. "He's a major ass about it, but it's his role to preside over and maintain the natural order. As much as I hate to say it, if there is anyone who knows what happened to your mom, it's that asinine grim reaper."

The only way Bennet's dislike for the Collector could have been made any more painfully obvious would've been if he'd started putting up signs and charging admission to rant about it. Based on Peter's cryptic to sever all ties to Bennet, even going as far as to call him an abomination that defied the natural order when he gave it to me, it felt safe to assume there was no love lost between them.

"Are you sure that's a good idea?" I asked, concerned that Bennet's petty feud with an apparent cosmic entity of death would only cause problems.

"It's better than fumbling blindly, looking for answers," he said. "If you'd like, we can go to the Collector's domain right now."

I took a deep breath, steeling my resolve. While I hadn't expected Bennet to give me any leads on my mother's death so suddenly, I was ready to seize the opportunity without hesitation. There was no way I'd get another chance like this.

"Alright, let's go," I declared. "No time like the present."

Bennet smirked, amused. "I like that fire in your eyes, Yuri," he said. "It suits you. Keep up that energy, because you're gonna need it."

#

Bennet escorted me to the foyer at the front of his cottage. He parted one of the intricate tapestries that hung by the entryway, revealing a full-body mirror behind it. It had an old and faded silver frame, and the glass was slightly scratched, the reflection itself almost smearing and indecipherable.

"This is a Travel Glass," Bennet said. "It's used to create portals to other areas within the Otherside. As long as you can picture where you're going, you can use it to go to any other Travel Glass you like on this side of reality."

Bennet approached the mirror. He breathed against the glass, fogging the reflection. With his usual dramatic flair, Bennet wrote "The Collector's Domain" in the condensation in neat cursive. The reflection distorted and warped, the image slowly transforming into something else entirely. Before I knew it, I was staring into an entryway that led to a place made entirely of glowing blue crystals.

"Shall we?" Bennet mused.

We entered through the archway to the Collector's domain. The entire landscape was made of glowing blue crystals that suspended themselves over a sea of darkness like floating islands. No sun, moon, or stars shone above. Below the giant crystal landmasses was a bottomless abyss. There was nothing to be seen below or above but never-ending darkness. The only source of light in this world was the crystals that made up the entirety of its terrain. It reminded me of winter. The Collector's domain had an eerie beauty to it, but one that felt cold. Barren. Almost painful to the touch. A delicate and beautiful sadness subtly suspended itself throughout the entire atmosphere.

"Welcome to the Collector's domain," Bennet chimes. "It's the closest place in existence to the Farside. We're essentially on the doorstep of what some call the great beyond."

I gazed breathlessly, still taking in the sheer volume and otherworldly nature of the place Bennet had whisked me away to.

"Where do we even begin to look for Peter?" I thought aloud, still marveling at the sight of the world around me. "This place is huge."

"It won't be long before he realizes we're here," Bennet said. "This is *his* domain, after all."

A small blue orb of light, no bigger than a golf ball, flew down from above and floated towards me.

"Um, hello," I stammered, flustered by the orb's sudden appearance.

The orb floated and circled me playfully, almost like a hummingbird fluttering around a flower as it tickled my skin. The orb radiated a gentle warmth. It felt like a cozy, inviting hug compared to this otherwise cold and depressing world.

"Looks like that uptight reaper knows we're here already," Bennet said. "He'll be here any second."

I jumped backward, startled by a blue blaze of fire that erupted a few feet away. The flames danced as

Peter emerged from them, the sparks fizzling and dying as he stepped forward. In his dark suit and black-rimmed glasses, Peter was just as I remembered from back during our first encounter. The coldness that he emanated was powerful and intimidating. If Peter were just a stranger on the street, and you told me that the man who currently stood before me was an avatar of death, I would have been inclined to believe you.

"Have I not told you many times before to never set foot in my domain?" Peter said, his voice as frigid and unfriendly as the glare he shot at Bennet.

Bennet sneered, the contempt in his eyes blatant enough for even a blind man five miles away to see. "Geez, Hades," he scoffed. "If this is how you greet people who visit you, it's no wonder everybody fears the reaper."

No description or metaphor I could think of could properly describe the sarcastic bite and venom in Bennet's tone as he referred to Peter as Hades.

"Enough with the pleasantries, Bennet," the Collector ordered. "What is it you want?"

"Come on now, four eyes," Bennet said. "No need to get your tie all knotted up over nothing."

"Easy for you to say, *abomination*," Peter replied coldly.

He placed a heavy, dramatic emphasis on "abomination." If looks could've actually killed, the glare that accompanied the quip would have demolished a small town.

"Right, right," Bennet grumbled flippantly. "Natural order this and natural order that. It'd be nice if you could learn some other topics for small talk."

Peter remained silent, choosing instead to direct his attention my way. He scanned me up and down, as if evaluating me.

"You've already met my assistant," Bennet said. "I brought him here because he has some questions that only you can answer, Mister Collector."

Peter stood silently, glaring coldly at Bennet while maintaining the best poker face I had ever seen.

"Be honest with yourself, Hades," he said mockingly. "I know you've been dying to get to know this one a little better. Now's the perfect chance."

Peter sighed. "Very well," he said. "I can spare my time for Mister Weissman. However, you will have to leave this instant."

Bennet scoffed, deridingly throwing his hands in the air in sarcastic defeat. "You don't have to tell me twice," he replied. "The mere sight of you is nauseating. I'd better get out of here before I spew all over the place."

"Wait, you're going?" I asked.

Bennet shrugged. "I knew he'd want me out of here the moment he saw me," he said. "It can't be helped."

"But I can't do this without you—"

"Yes, you can, Yuri," Bennet interjected. "I wouldn't have brought you here in the first place if I didn't think you could."

He placed his hand on my shoulder, the firm and gentle touch steadying my mind before it began to race.

"You wanted answers, and this is your best shot," Bennet said. "I know you don't want to miss an opportunity. You'll always regret it if you do."

I silently nodded, knowing full well there was no arguing with Bennet this time. I would have never gotten a better chance to learn the truth behind my mom's death than this moment, right here and now. There was no way I could squander it because I was afraid. Bennet patted my shoulder.

"I'll keep an eye on you through my charm," he said. "Stay safe out there."

Bennet sauntered back to the Travel Glass from which he and I had arrived, turning over his shoulder to address Peter before he departed. "Be good to my assistant," he said coldly. "If anything happens to him while he's here, there will be hell to pay. You got that?"

Peter said nothing in response to Bennet's threat as he departed. I was now standing in a strange world with a cosmic entity of death, whom Bennet mockingly referred to as Hades, as my only company. I had no idea what to expect from that point onward, but I needed to be prepared for anything. I was going to do whatever it took to get the answers I had been searching for.

CHAPTER 17

THE COLLECTOR

Silence. If I had to describe the domain of the Collector in one word, that word would've been silence. The quiet was so overwhelming that it felt like standing in a barren tundra. As a result, I found the subtle sound of crystals crunching under my feet like snow a blessing.

Peter's gaze was stone-faced as he evaluated me. It was a mystery to me what to say or how to act around him. My inability to read his stoic expression made the situation all the more complicated and uncomfortable. I wouldn't have been able to tell you what he was thinking about, even if my life had actively depended on it. That's why it surprised me when Peter was the one to speak first.

"Let's go to a better place to talk," he said while straightening his glasses.

Peter snapped his fingers. We were both instantly enveloped in blue flames, obscuring my vision as they danced around me, prickling my skin with their cold touch. When the blue embers dispersed, I found myself sitting in a chair across from Peter with a small table between us. We sat in a gazebo—also made of the blue crystal—that looked upon an open stretch of the same material, like it were a field of flowers. The table between us and the chairs we sat in were also made of the blue crystals, and they crunched quietly as I shifted my weight.

Two blue orbs like the one from earlier floated down from above. One of them delivered a tea set that looked like a priceless antique. The orb carefully placed a cup in front of me and another in front of Peter before setting a steaming teapot on the table. The second orb placed a small bowl of sugar and a small pitcher of cream next to the teapot. The first orb then proceeded to pick up the teapot and pour its contents into the cups. Not once in my life had I ever thought an avatar of death would spirit me away for a tea party.

"Milk and sugar for you?" Peter asked, his tone flat.

"I'm good," I replied bluntly.

The Collector quietly sipped from his cup while I observed the orbs that floated around us. I'd heard a lot about myths and folktales involving the underworld and how consuming food there typically ended terribly for those who visited. I decided I'd rather not potentially risk experiencing those stories firsthand.

Instead, I watched the little blue orbs of light that seemed to do Peter's bidding.

"What are those things?" I asked.

"They're wisps," Peter replied, "Others that reside here and guide departed souls to the Farside, where they await rebirth. They act as emissaries and messengers on my behalf. They're instrumental to the role that I play."

"And they serve you tea. How sweet," I scoffed while rolling my eyes.

Peter took another sip from his cup before gently setting it back down on the table. "You fascinate me, Yuri Weissman," he said.

Unless he was speaking about Bennet, Peter always used the same flat tone regardless of the topic of discussion. It was yet another reason why reading him was all the more difficult.

"Care to elaborate?" I asked.

"It is quite far from unheard of for humans to have near-death experiences," he explained. "Yet your soul was quite… unique in that regard."

My eyes narrowed. "You mean when I almost died as a kid," I said, glaring.

"Yes," Peter replied. "Usually, when a soul makes contact with the Farside, it is unable to return to the realm of the living without being reborn. Yet your soul returned at the last possible moment, as if something had called it back to where it once came."

"Is that a big deal?" I asked.

It was subtle, but I saw Peter's eyes flicker with interest ever so slightly. "Has Bennet not told you how human mages derive their power?" he asked.

"Only that it originates from the Farside or something," I replied.

"Typical," he muttered to himself, annoyed.

Peter held out his hand, conjuring a small blue flame in his palm.

"Others derive their power from nature. Their natural ties to the Otherside and the Nearside allow them to use magic as easily as they draw breath. Humans are quite different in that regard."

Peter crushed the flame in his clenched fist, smoke smoldering from between his knuckles.

"Human mages instead derive their power from an innate connection to the Farside," Peter said. "It is a connection that few humans are naturally born with, and it requires a great deal of time and training to master and properly utilize that natural link."

He took another sip from his teacup before he continued speaking. "I suspect that it was your prior contact with the Farside that has enabled your innate potential," he said. "That brief moment altered the very nature of your soul in a way that, quite frankly, I have never seen before."

I was starting to understand and sympathize with Bennet's contempt for Peter the more I interacted with him.

"Do you have to be so casual about it?" I spat, "That change wasn't exactly sunshine and daisies, and that's setting aside the fact I almost died that day. My dad died that day, for crying out loud! Would it kill you to at least fake a little empathy or not be such a dick about it?"

"You sound like Bennet," Peter mused.

His eyes narrowed like those of a cunning snake. It surprised me he didn't wear some sort of sadistic smirk or sneer to accompany the look.

"Death is the one thing every living creature has in common," he said. "No matter who you are or what you do, life delivers everyone equally to the same end."

The way Peter talked about death and the natural order made him sound like some heartless tax collector performing an intense audit.

"Bennet takes issue with my pragmatic outlook, even after attempting to meddle with forces far beyond his understanding," he said.

I recalled the shame I saw in Bennet whenever the topic of his past came up. *Is what Peter's referring to the source of that shame?* I contemplated to myself.

"What was it that Bennet did?" I asked.

"I'm not at liberty to discuss such things," Peter said coldly.

For a moment, I thought I felt a blood vessel in my brain pop from sheer frustration. "Of course you aren't," I replied dryly.

It annoyed me that both Bennet and Peter had such a penchant for cryptic answers. It was probably the one thing they had in common. They would prattle on about some vague or profound event from Bennet's past, only to shut up entirely before they revealed anything of actual substance. I stewed in that petty frustration as I shot a dirty look at Peter. He paid it no mind as he took another sip of tea from his cup.

"Bennet said you had a request of me," Peter said. "What is it? My time is quite valuable."

"I'm trying to get answers about how my mom died," I said. "Bennet said you would be the best person to ask."

"Ah, yes," Peter replied. "Evelyn Angela Weissman." He tilted his head slightly. "You were there to witness her death, were you not?"

"That's not what I'm referring to!" I replied, barely restraining my frustration. "A Specter had come to haunt her—a Demon Parasite, to be precise. It should have driven her to kill me, but instead, she was the one who died. I want to know why."

"I know why," Peter said.

"Are you gonna tell me? Or is it just another thing you don't have the liberty to discuss?" I asked mockingly.

The Collector stood up, moving to stand behind me before placing his hand on my clavicle. He leaned down and whispered into my ear, speaking almost like he was a devil on my shoulder.

"Are you sure you want to know?" he asked, his voice soft and gentle. "The truth could be far worse than you could ever imagine. Are you prepared for such a thing? Perhaps it's best you leave some mysteries unsolved."

Peter's breath was cold against my skin. His voice and words were like those of a cult leader coyly tempting me with the idea that ignorance is bliss.

"After all, what does it matter?" he asked. "Knowing the truth won't bring her back."

I stood up. "It matters because I want to know!" I retorted in a shout. "I already made up my mind! I won't look away from the truth anymore!"

Peter dropped his hand from my shoulder and slumped for a moment before slowly returning to his original seat. He took another sip of his tea, gently placing the cup on the table, quietly clearing his throat.

"Very well. I will give you the knowledge you seek," Peter said. "If you can first prove to me your resolve."

I felt a sinking feeling in my gut about what was to come next. "What do you mean?" I asked.

"Ordinarily, I wouldn't be at liberty to discuss such things," Peter said. "But I'm quite curious about your potential. Complete the task I assign you, and I'll provide the information you desire."

"And that task is?" I asked, bracing myself for anything.

Peter clasped his hands together and placed them on the table as he leaned in. It reminded me of an executive on some TV drama giving a business proposal.

"This place is the closest part of the realm of the living to the Farside," Peter said. "All souls must make the journey through here to reach the Farside, where they all will await rebirth."

"Can you get to the point already?" I snapped.

Peter straightened his glasses, almost as if to say, "I'm getting there."

"Many times, when a soul makes their way through my domain, they carry with them the regrets they had moments before their death," he said. "These regrets form the lesser Specters classified as Ghouls. When left unchecked, they can do a great deal of damage to my domain and even endanger the various souls during their pilgrimage home to the Farside."

Despite Peter's stoic expression, his gaze was intense and serious as he looked directly into my eyes.

"There is a ghoul that is currently wreaking havoc in an area deeper within my domain," he said. "Exorcise it all on your own, without any assistance from Bennet, and I will give you any information about your mother that you desire."

I bit my lip slightly, already feeling myself instinctively recoil at the prospect of Peter's proposal.

"I've never exorcised a Specter that wasn't already restrained by magic or a seal," I said.

"As I said before, my time is quite valuable," Peter said. "Those are my terms. Fulfill my request and prove to me your resolve, or leave now and don't ever return."

Peter once again passively-aggressively straightened his glasses. "It's a reasonable trade, is it not?" he asked. "So tell me, what is your answer to my proposal?"

I clenched my fists. I had no idea if I had what it took to stand up to a Specter in my current state. I could very easily get myself killed if I wasn't careful. The thought terrified me. I didn't want to die. Not yet. But what terrified me even more than dying was running away from this opportunity and spending the rest of my life regretting it.

"I'll do it," I said. "I'll exorcise that Specter and prove to you that I am serious about this."

A faint smile crept over Peter's lips. I was almost knocked over from surprise at the sight of it.

"Very well," he said. "I'll have a wisp guide you to the area where the Ghoul was last sighted. The Ghouls that appear here sustain themselves by devouring souls directly, so they'll be much stronger than their usual kin. Do try to be careful."

One of the wisps that brought us the tea from earlier returned, floating down from above to greet me as it did. Peter stood up from his chair.

"Escort Mister Weissman to the Gamma Quadrant where the Ghoul was last spotted, and monitor his progress," Peter said to the wisp.

The wisp swayed slightly, as if nodding in affirmation to Peter's orders.

"The Gamma Quadrant is an isolated segment of my domain," Peter said. "The ghoul will be unable to leave that isle in its current state. This wisp will guide you there. Best of luck, Yuri Weissman."

In an instant, Peter was enveloped in blue flames and vanished in the crackling embers as quickly as they appeared. The wisp that was assigned as my guide bobbed and weaved in the direction of the open field of crystals, a short distance away from the gazebo Peter had spirited me away to.

"Do you want me to follow you that way?" I asked.

The wisp's light flickered slightly in confirmation.

"Lead the way then."

CHAPTER 18

THE STRANGE WORLD HAUNTED

BY A GHOUL

With the wisp as my guide, we traversed the wide-open crystal plane. The crystals crunched my feet like snow, leaving faint indentations from my shoes as I journeyed onward into this strange place. The Collector's domain was a dark world, and the blue glow of the crystal landmasses and wisps were the only things in this place that felt warm or inviting, like something could live here. The melancholy and surreal atmosphere felt fitting for a place that was supposed to act as the border between life and death.

As I embarked on my assigned trial, other wisps would occasionally float down from above and observe me curiously.

The only sound that any of them made was like the chiming of a small bell. Otherwise, they seemed to communicate by flickering, like they were speaking in a combination of Morse code and floating in a specific motion.

Without a sun in the sky, it felt impossible to tell how much time had passed since Bennet dropped me off here. The wisp Peter assigned as my guide beckoned me to the edge of this crystal land mass. The crystalline isle's cliff edge gave way to a wide open view of several crystal landmasses floating off in the distant darkness, and falling off the edge would have spelled certain doom.

"How am I supposed to cross?" I asked. "I can't fly like you can."

The wisp quietly chimed as if to say, "I understand." It floated off the edge of the isle, and small chunks of crystal started materializing underneath it, forming a path like stepping stones that descended downward.

The wisp flickered several times, this time as if to say, "Watch your step."

I took a deep breath, trying not to look down as I followed the pathway the wisp created for me. We descended downward, with the path sculpting itself into a crystalline staircase as I marched onward.

The wisp and I had probably journeyed the equivalent of seven city blocks when I stepped off the conjured path and onto a new landmass of crystals. The Gamma Quadrant, as Peter called it, felt different from the other part of his domain I'd visited. A subtle and inexplicable tension lingered in the area. There were mounds and pillars of crystals that gave off no light, dull and grey instead. Each of these structures bore heavy gouges and slashes like something had clawed and gnawed away at them in a blind rage.

I pulled Bennet's charm from my pocket and held it up by the leather string.

"You're still watching, right, Bennet?" I said.

"Haven't missed a moment. You've had me on the edge the whole time," he replied. "Nice job sticking it to Hades earlier."

"So you already know about the trial that Peter set out for me," I said.

"I wouldn't have suggested you visit him if I didn't think you could handle yourself," Bennet said.

I kneeled and examined the damaged crystals. "Is there anything you can tell me about Ghouls that appear here?" I asked. "This one seems a lot stronger than the smaller ones you have me practice on."

"It has to do with the very nature of the Collector's Domain," Bennet said. "Premature death is a tremendous source of despair—that goes without saying. In their final moments, people's lives flash before their eyes. They bemoan their parting regrets and almost always curse this cruel world and their unjust fates. This despair suffered in their final moments gives birth to Specters, and without a host to haunt, they end up as Ghouls that mindlessly roam the Collector's domain with an insatiable hunger that can be quelled by a singular means there."

I gasped in horror. "You don't mean—"

"Yes," Bennet said. "They feed on the souls in the process of returning to the Farside. Souls flow through the crystals that make up the Collector's domain like a lifeblood, after all."

I took in the sights around me once more. It dawned on me why the crystals here were the only source of light and land in this cold and dark domain. Aside from the wisps and Peter who presided over them, these structures were the only source of life in this place. Without them, the Collector's domain would be a dark abyss of silence—and nothing more.

"Be careful, Yuri," Bennet said. "This Specter that Hades has tasked you with hunting is a Ghoul in name only. It will still be relatively powerful and will put up a fight. Stay safe out there, and best of luck."

The glow from Bennet's charm faded, and I was once again left alone with the wisp who'd guided me here. I could feel Peter's trial now take on a heavier weight as I placed the charm back into my pocket. While I was still intent on getting answers about my mother from Peter, I also had another important reason to see this through.

I won't let any more souls come to harm, I thought to myself. *I will stop that Ghoul.*

I once again addressed my wisp guide.

"Do you know where the Ghoul is now?" I asked.

The wisp flickered, swaying in a way that resembled someone shaking their head no.

"I didn't think so," I said. "That's okay."

I knelt once more to examine the gouges that had been left behind by the Ghoul. It would've been a terrible idea to wander blindly in a place with a Specter prowling about. Bennet had said that the Ghouls here are usually born from the despair someone felt right before they died.

Would it be possible for me to use Resonance to track that despair? I contemplated to myself.

"Here's goes nothing…" I thought aloud.

I never invoked Resonance intentionally before. I took a deep breath before tracing my fingers over the gouges. With each breath I took, I tried to empty and clear my mind. Almost on instinct, I closed my eyes.

"*It hurts,*" I heard a small boy's voice cry weakly.

In my mind, I could see bright red flames dancing violently as an overwhelming sense of fear and sadness washed over me.

"Everything hurts," the voice echoed weakly. *"Where are mom and dad? Why won't anyone save me?"*

Flames fully enveloped my vision.

"Am I going to die?" the boy's voice echoed.

I opened my eyes, trembling slightly at what I had seen and heard. It was a child's final moments. He was afraid and in pain. The flames in my vision left very little to the imagination; the boy's cause of death was painfully obvious. He was young enough that he didn't even fully understand what was happening. I clenched my fist, punching into the ground. It was all so fucked up. Why did the world have to be like this? This boy didn't even get a chance to live his life!

I took a deep breath, trying to calm down my emotions. It was on me now to put the boy's regrets to rest. Failure wasn't an option. I stood up, straining my ears for the slightest sound.

"It hurts," the boy's voice echoed quietly in the distance. *"Someone save me."*

"Come on," I said to the Wisp. "It's this way."

#

The crystals had started to rise from the ground like a labyrinth as I tracked down the Ghoul. They wrapped around themselves intricately like blown glass, glowing brightly as I ventured onward with my wisp companion. The boy's voice continued to cry in pain, growing louder as we got closer to the source of the sound. The further we trekked, the more and more crystal formations bore deep gouges and slashes, rendering them dull and grey. Some formations had been shattered completely, the remains scattered on the ground like broken glass.

"Why won't anyone save me?" the boy's voice echoed. *"I don't wanna die!"*

We were close now. The sense of dread in the air was so palpable that it almost felt stagnant. It was a sense of foreboding that only a Specter could bring about.

At last, the Wisp and I emerged from the labyrinth into a wide-open clearing where small blue crystal shards rose from the ground like flowers. I could see something a short distance away, hunched over, gouging and eating the crystals beneath.

Calling it a "thing" would have been generous. The Ghoul was only vaguely humanoid, with waxy, grey skin—like decaying human flesh. It was heavily muscled, like a feral beast, and its size would have easily dwarfed a normal human.

The wisp who'd accompanied me flickered weakly before hiding behind me. Despite its lack of facial expression, I could easily discern the fear the wisp felt at the mere sight of our quarry.

The ghoul stopped eating abruptly, rising slowly, turning its head. It had no eyes or ears. Its only facial feature was a large mouth with too many fangs that drooled a black sludge. The Ghoul twitched erratically.

"It hurts!" it cried in the boy's voice. "I don't wanna die!"

It was like the Ghoul was in pain from its very existence. I clenched my fists, steeling my resolve for what had to be done.

"I will free you from your suffering," I declared.

CHAPTER 19

MEMENTO MORI

The Ghoul roared, lunging at me like a leopard. I dug my heels into the ground, raising my hands upward, and outstretched them towards the ghoul. I could practically hear Bennet's words in my ears as I recalled how he described magic.

"Magic, at its apex, is the ability to create a miracle."

My resolve was set, the magic swirling within me as naturally as my beating heart pumping blood into my veins.

"Why does it hurt?" the Ghoul cried. "I don't wanna die!"

The Ghoul charged, picking up speed. The wisp behind me quivered in fear against my back. The Ghoul lept upward with a powerful pounce into the sky, barreling full force at me.

Failure isn't an option; I will see this through. I thought to myself in affirmation.

The words for my incantation came to my lips like instinct.

"Oh, mournful sorrow and pain that clings to this world!" I called. "I relieve you of your burden! Be free from this reality and haunt it no longer!"

The Ghoul froze in midair, screeching as light burst from within. It screeched and howled before erupting into a flash of light that scattered like fireflies.

"Thank you…" the boy's voice whispered.

I gazed upon the light as it scattered and faded away.

"I hope you find happiness in your next life," I said.

I heard the sound of someone slowly clapping their hands.

"Well done," Peter called.

The Collector sat upon a crystal formation that rose from the ground behind me.

"How long have you been there?" I asked.

"I've been observing you the whole time," Peter said. He got to his feet. "You truly are remarkable. I suppose it's time that I held up my end of the bargain."

#

Peter whisked me away back to the crystalline gazebo, where we'd sat down for tea when I first arrived. The reality of what I had accomplished still hadn't sunk in. It was the first time I'd exorcised a Specter like that, but it didn't feel like anything special to me anymore. All I wanted to do was set free that boy's despair so his soul could rest peacefully. I should have been proud of myself, but instead, I was left with a sour taste in my mouth.

"You've impressed me, Yuri Weissman," Peter said. "Your potential exceeds all of my expectations."

"It doesn't feel like something worth celebrating, if I'm being honest," I replied. "I know it was only the regrets he left behind, but..."

I frowned, averting my eyes from Peter.

"He was just a kid," I said. "Call it bad luck or fate, or whatever else. He never got a chance to live his life. It's unfair that he had to die the way he did."

Peter sighed. Despite retaining his usual stoic expression, he couldn't hide the melancholy in his eyes.

"I lost track of how many times I've heard sentiments like that long ago," he said.

It surprised me. His sadness was subtle, but this was probably the first time I'd witnessed something so distinctly human from Peter.

"My directive is a simple one," he said. "Guide the souls of the departed to the next realm so that they can await rebirth, and collect and record their names and the circumstances that led to their demise. It is the natural order. There cannot be renewal without decay.

It is a tragic reality, but all things must come to an end."

I couldn't deny the harsh truth in Peter's words.

"Many people die filled with despair and regret, Yuri Weissman," Peter said. "Life can easily be summed up as a journey marching to your own grave. How those lives meet their ends may differ, but that end always arrives sooner or later, nonetheless. The most anyone can do with the gift of life is make the most of what they have while they still can."

"You're right," I replied quietly. "I'm sorry for being so hostile with you before."

I could only imagine the countless tragedies Peter had to record because of his role in this world. It was slightly comforting to know that, as hardened and callous as he was, Peter had not become as desensitized to that gravitas as I had assumed.

The Collector held out his hand. A blue burst of flame appeared, and from the embers emerged a small black folder. On the front of it was a white label with "Evelyn Angela Weissman" written in a charcoal sans serif font. Peter placed the folder down on the table in front of me.

"You honored your end of the bargain, so I will honor mine," he said. "Before we continue, though, I must ask: are you certain you are prepared?"

I closed my eyes, taking a deep breath to steady my nerves and steel my resolve once more.

"You said it yourself," I replied. "Mortals only have one life to live, and the best they can do is to make the most of the time they do have. I know if I go my entire life always running away from what happened that day, I'll never be able to heal from it. I'll regret it until the day I die."

"Very well," Peter said.

He cleared his throat, once again taking on the facade of a detached emissary of death he was known for.

"Your mother was indeed possessed by the Specter classified as a Daemon Parasite," Peter said. "As you know, the Daemon Parasite pushes its victims to commit the most vile of atrocities. It erodes their willpower until they are mindless husks. No matter how hard a victim may try to resist the influence of the Daemon Parasite, without someone like you or Bennet to remove it, or the Parasite voluntarily relinquishing its control, submitting to its sway is an inevitable fate."

"You mean—" I stammered.

"You were powerless to exorcise that Specter from her," Peter said. "And while she held onto her sense of self for a remarkably long time, the Parasite would have inevitably driven her mad. There was nothing you could have done to save her."

Peter's words twisted and coiled around my chest like a rope.

"Why was she the one to die then?" I asked.

"Your mother eventually came to realize something was amiss," Peter said. "She was becoming painfully aware of the vile intent blossoming in her heart. The desire for your death beckoned her like a siren's song."

I sat breathlessly, my entire being focused on Peter's voice.

"It terrified her," he said. "'What kind of mother would want to kill her own son?' she thought to herself."

"Then why didn't she kill me?" I cried. "Why..."
Peter paused.

"Because her love for you was stronger," he said. "She'd sooner die than do anything to hurt the child she loved with her entire heart."

I stared in stunned disbelief, emotionally paralyzed by the revelation. Peter pushed the folder across the table with his left hand.

"Touch the folder, Yuri," Peter said. "With the Resonance you possess, you will hear her final thoughts before she died. Hear them for yourself."

I reached for the folder, my hand trembling. I gulped. Pushing through the torrent of emotions welling up within me, I placed the tips of my fingers on the folder and closed my eyes.

"I'm so sorry for leaving you like this, Yuri," my mom's voice echoed in my head. *"I can't stop this awful impulse in my mind. It's relentless. It won't go away. I'm terrified there will come a time when I can't stop myself any longer. I won't ask you to forgive me for what I did to you today. I just hope that you'll one day be able to open your heart and cherish the life you have. I'm sorry, Yuri…I'm sorry I couldn't be a better mother to you."*

"Mom…" I trembled.

"Yuri…" my mom's voice echoed. *"I love you."*

I opened my eyes, my throat choked up from the sadness I felt.

"If it's any consolation, Yuri," Peter said. "Your mother's soul did make the journey back to the Farside. She will be reborn one day. Her soul still carries on."

I looked down at my feet. "Good," I choked. "I'm glad…"

Peter stood up and slowly walked over, gently placing his hand on my shoulder. "I'll give you a moment to absorb everything you've heard," he said. "Take all the time you need."

Peter walked away, the faint glow of blue flames appearing behind me as he vanished.

I couldn't contain it anymore. Tears streamed down my face. Every burden I had carried with me from that fateful day, every bottled-up emotion, came tumbling out. The sounds of my despair echoed in the silence as I wept. It was bittersweet. The wounds in my heart cut deep. The feeling was raw and volatile, but I finally felt the burden I carried get just a little lighter in that moment.

I could finally start to heal.

\#

I emerged from the Travel Glass in Bennet's house. Peter escorted me back after I finished crying, though it would have been more accurate to say I had run out of tears. It was all a lot to take in—learning that there was nothing I could have done to save my mom, how long she'd resisted the Daemon Parasite's influence, that she ultimately chose my life over her own. It was heart-wrenching, and that was putting it mildly.

Still, I didn't regret learning the truth. I knew I never would.

If I hadn't risen to Peter's challenge, I would've spent the rest of my life wasting away, constantly questioning if I'd made the right decision or not. I knew it was the right decision, but in that moment, it didn't ease the pain I felt.

"Welcome back, Yuri," Bennet called from down the hall.

Without calling back, I turned and walked to the usual sitting area. Bennet was already seated upright on one of the couches, legs crossed, his hands clasped in his lap.

"You did a great job," he said. "As your teacher, I couldn't be any prouder of you. You really are incredible."

"It wasn't anything special," I said, sitting down on the opposite couch. "I wouldn't have been able to do it if it weren't for you."

"Take the compliment," Bennet scoffed. "All I did was point you in the right direction. It was ultimately your resolve and power that got the job done."

Bennet sighed, uncrossing his legs and reclining on the couch. "If I'm being honest," he said with a wry smile. "I'm actually a little jealous of you."

I was dumbfounded by Bennet's statement. "Why would you be jealous of me?" I asked, my eyes wide with disbelief.

"You and I are more alike than you think," he said. "There was someone I cared about and lost a long time ago, too."

Bennet slouched, placing his elbow on the couch's arm and resting his head on the back of his hand. "Agnes," he said. "That was her name. It was so long ago that it might as well have been a different life entirely."

"Who was she?" I asked.

"She was the woman I loved," Bennet said. "I thought I'd spend the rest of my life with her."

Despite his smile, the melancholy was abundantly clear in Bennet's voice, his eyes glassy as he painfully reminisced.

"Fate had other plans, though," he said. "Agnes was born with a weak heart and ultimately died before we were supposed to get married."

"I'm sorry," I said, almost on reflex.

Bennet shook his head. "Don't be," he said. "There was nothing anyone could have done. It's in the past now."

He looked into my eyes, his melancholy clear as daybreak despite his unbroken smile. It was a pain I understood intimately as well.

"You're far stronger than I am, Yuri," Bennet said.

"You're joking, right?" I replied.

Bennet shook his head.

"Your strength goes beyond your potential with magic," he said. "You're honest, and you're stubborn. It's that kind of willpower that's gotten you so far in the past few months. Even when you're afraid or unsure, you push on anyway. I'm not like that."

I grimaced, feeling undeserving of Bennet's praise. "You're giving me too much credit," I said. "When you found me, I was a miserable mess trying desperately to live a normal life. I'm not strong, or brave, or honest, or anything like that."

"Again, Yuri," Bennet said. "All I did was point you in the right direction. While there were moments I encouraged you to go down a certain path, every decision and every accomplishment you've made was done so out of your own free will. That strength has always been inside you."

It felt foreign to me, being praised like this. It wasn't that I hated the feeling, but I also felt like I didn't deserve it. No one had ever said something like that about me before. What felt even more foreign, though, was how open Bennet was being with me. Maybe this was the best time to ask a question that'd been burning in the back of my skull for a while now.

"Hey, Bennet," I said sheepishly. "What happened between Peter and you? Why are you guys always at each other's throats all the time?"

Bennet shrugged. "I figured you'd ask about that sooner or later," he said.

The smile on his face finally vanished.

"I promise I'm not trying to keep anything from you," he said. "It's more so I have a hard time talking about it out loud."

"What is it?" I asked.

Bennet looked away in shame.

"It's something I'm not proud of," he said. "I was young and foolish, and I ended up making a mistake a long time ago that fills me with shame to this very day. Peter has held it against me for a long time as well."

He sighed. "Truth be told, I don't blame him," Bennet confessed. "That being said, seeing his stupid face always reminds me of my mistake every time. It angers me."

Bennet returned his gaze to me. "My motivation for taking up my old teacher's mantle was so I could atone for what I've done," he said darkly. "But, I've been wondering lately if the work I do is nothing more than a temporary balm. I'm afraid Specters and Malevolence will one day tear apart all reality as we know it, and there will be nothing I can do to stop it. That all I've ever done is delay the inevitable."

Bennet grimaced. "I'm sorry," he said. "I don't want to talk about it anymore."

"I'm sorry, too," I said. "I didn't mean to open up old wounds."

Without missing a beat, Bennet flashed me the same casual, devil-may-care expression that had almost become synonymous with my image of him.

"It's alright," he said. "All we can do is keep moving forward."

I thought I understood Bennet a little better then. He put on a brave face, but he was just as haunted by his past as I was by mine. While he probably only said it to mask his true feelings, Bennet was right that the only thing we can do is live and keep moving forward. We all only have one life to live, so we must make the most of every moment, because life moves on with or without you.

CHAPTER 20

THE RAIN SPRITE'S REQUEST

My mom passed away a few weeks after my sixteenth birthday. Every year, no matter how busy or tired she was, she'd always go out of her way to make me a cake. She was never good at baking and often made do with a store-bought cake mix and frosting. Despite that, I always remember that cloying, artificial sweetness fondly.

"Make a wish," my mom said.

I smiled weakly, blowing out the lit one and six candles placed on the cake. I didn't make a wish. I'd stopped believing in such things by then. That said, I wanted to humor my mom. She went through so much trouble that it was only right that I met her halfway.

"You don't have to do all this, you know," I said. "It's your day off. You work hard enough for me as is."

My mom took the candles out of the cake before using a large knife to cut a slice. "I don't have to, but I want to," she replied.

I briefly glanced at the jet-black canary perched on her shoulder. "Why won't you give in and kill him already?" it said. "The boy is a burden who holds you back."

I sighed. "Are you sure it's no trouble?" I asked.

My mom smiled, sliding a plate with a slice of cake on it in front of me. "Absolutely sure," she said. "I like doing these things for you."

I could see a slight pained nostalgia in my mom's eyes as she gazed into mine. "You're looking more and more like your father every day," she said wistfully.

I looked away, digging my fork into the slice of cake. The store-bought frosting was sweet and sticky in my mouth.

"You're almost through high school now," my mom said. "Have you given any thought to what you might wanna do after you graduate?"

I placed my fork on the table. "Not really," I replied.

She smiled weakly. "That's fine."

"That's fine, but…" I said, sensing the apprehension in her tone.

She took a deep breath, staring out our apartment window and into the setting sun.

"We all only have one life to live, Yuri," she said. "Sometimes I get worried about you. That's all. Sometimes, I'm afraid you'll forget to enjoy life until it's too late."

"How am I supposed to live my life then?" I asked.

"There's no one answer, Yuri," my mom said. "There's no one right way to live a life. I just hope that whatever path you take, you live without regrets, okay?"

"Okay…" I replied, almost reluctantly.

#

Winter had come and gone. It felt like the blink of an eye, as late December turned into January, and time marched onward to late March. I started the spring semester without any problems and balanced my time between my coursework—with Amy often holding me to task about getting my assignments done—and assisting Bennet. He hadn't received any new requests in the past few weeks, but our hands were still full purifying various Abscesses that manifested in the Otherside.

That March Saturday afternoon carried on sluggishly.

My textbook was strewn open on my table as I attempted to take notes on various terms for an art history class I was taking for common core credit. It was hard to focus, especially with the warm, early spring sunshine outside taunting me as I studied. I tapped my foot, getting restless as I carried on.

Eventually, I couldn't take it anymore. I sighed, pushing my textbook away and letting out a groan as I slouched in my chair.

What was the point of all this? What was I doing all of this for?

I had almost made it through my sophomore year of college, and I still had to pick a major by next semester. If I wanted to keep going to Clover, I would also need to pick up a part-time job sooner or later to keep up with rent. My mom's last wish was that I live my life without regrets, but what was it I wanted to get out of life?

I had never thought about it until now. I'd only moved out here because it was the easiest way to get away from my aunt, uncle, and grandmother.

A loud tapping against my apartment window yanked me out of my thoughts. The sound of rain pouring outside was as constant as it was loud. I looked out the window and was caught off-guard by the sight outside. The downpour almost looked torrential, yet there wasn't a single cloud in the sky. Thinking about it, I hadn't even seen anything about rain in the weather forecast for this week.

There was a knock on my door. I got up from my chair and went to look through the peephole. I saw the vague outline of a girl I had never seen before. She knocked again.

"I'm looking for the human known as Yuri Weissman," she declared.

I gulped, knowing all too well that this girl was more than likely an Other. I opened my door, preparing myself for anything.

"You…" the girl said. "Are you the human known as Yuri Weissman?"

She had dark black hair and was wearing a grey zip-up hoodie while holding a black umbrella as she stood in the rain. Her face was sullen, her eyes weary and coldly shrewd. Her pale, smooth skin reminded me of a porcelain doll.

"Why are you looking for him?" I asked.

The girl stood motionless outside my doorway. "I need him to take me to the human known as Bennet Grey," she said. "Are you Yuri Weissman or not?"

From the corner of my eye, I could see the faint green glow of Bennet's charm on the folding table next to my bed.

"It's okay, Yuri," Bennet's voice called. "Escort her to the Otherside. We can chat there."

#

After rushed introductions and explanations, I escorted the girl through my apartment door and to Bennet's home in the Otherside. She had placed her dripping wet umbrella on the ground of the foyer when we entered, and I escorted her to the usual sitting room. Rain poured outside, mixed with the fluttering petals of cherry blossoms. The girl sat on the couch opposite Bennet. I stood behind him, still somewhat apprehensive about her potential motives for seeking him out.

"It's not every day I get a request from a rain sprite," Bennet said. "If a literal force of nature is asking for my assistance, the circumstances must be dire."

The girl stared coldly back at Bennet. "You can call me Undine," she said. "And yes, my need is quite urgent."

"Care to elaborate?" Bennet mused.

Undine pouted in response. "For the record, I hate humans," she spat. "Humans are parasites that destroy nature and wipe their asses with its bounty. The fact that I have to take on this form so I can communicate with you makes me want to find a hole to crawl in and die."

I couldn't say I blamed Undine for her outlook, and I probably would have felt the same in her shoes. Her sentiment still stung, though.

"Then why seek assistance from the humans you loathe so much?" Bennet asked dryly.

Undine crossed her arms, irritably looking away from him. "Circumstances being as they are, I don't have the luxury of clinging to my pride as a nature spirit."

"What's wrong?" I asked. "What can we do to help?"

Undine frowned, all but sighing in defeat as she finally let herself open up. "There's an area of land I typically preside over. It's about twenty miles away from your abode, Yuri Weissman."

"Did something happen?" I asked.

Undine nodded. "There's a dark curse that floats above the skies there," she said. "It brings about an unnatural, perpetual rain that now plagues the area."

"A rain sprite asking me to stop a rainstorm," Bennet thought aloud. "How ironic."

"That rainstorm is unnatural," Undine said darkly. "Blighted, to be precise."

She practically clenched her elbows as she crossed her arms. "The raindrops bring about a miasma that slowly kills the land in the area. If the storm continues any longer, the living creatures there will start to fall ill to the plague it brings. The land itself will begin to rot away as the corruption continues to spread."

"Do you have any idea what this cursed rain's source might be?" Bennet asked.

Undine nodded. "The source is a woman called Emma Thompson," she said. "It is she who invited that cursed blight into this world. I've heard whispers of a human who specialized in such matters, so here I am."

Bennet clasped his hands in his lap. "Very well, Undine," he said. "I will take your request."

The rain sprite stood up. "I don't come seeking the assistance of humans lightly," she said. "It's in everyone's best interest that this threat is conquered as swiftly as possible. Do not fail me."

Without even saying goodbye, Undine walked away. I could hear the door closing as she grabbed her umbrella and left the Otherside. As soon as she departed, the rain ceased almost instantly.

"What's the plan of attack, Bennet?" I asked.

Bennet yawned before lounging his feet on the coffee table in front of him, reclining his back on the couch as he looked back up at me. "I'll survey the area she spoke of first thing tomorrow to get a better picture of exactly what we're dealing with," he said. "Perhaps Amy can help you track down information on this Emma Thompson that Undine mentioned."

"Okay," I replied.

It was in that moment that I saw the dark shadows that had formed under his eyes. "Are you sure you're up for this, Bennet?" I asked.

He nodded.

"I have a job to do, Yuri," he said. "The only thing that matters is that I get it done."

I could sense that Bennet was hurting. Something had just been off about him since he mentioned Agnes and being jealous of me. That said, I knew that pressing him on it would have made him push me away harder. All I could do was support him the best I could with the request we had just received. I owed Bennet so much, and all I wanted was to help him the same way he had helped me.

CHAPTER 21

CARPE DIEM

I sat in the coffee house I usually met Amy at for our regular study sessions, having already picked up a chai latte and a blonde roast that I'd ordered for Amy and myself. I'd texted her the night before, asking for her help after filling her in on all the information Undine gave Bennet and me. I was sure Bennet would be alright studying the rainstorm, but I couldn't shake this feeling deep down that something terrible was going to happen.

Perhaps I'm just being paranoid. He'll probably use his charm to reach out to me whenever he needs it, I assured myself in deep thought.

Bennet hadn't been himself since he reluctantly shared his past with me back in December, and I was starting to get a little worried. Even when we were getting a request from Undine, he seemed more somber than normal.

The faint buzz of people talking nearby and the din of baristas preparing orders from behind the counter filled the air as I sat, lost in my thoughts. I rested my head in my hand, staring out a nearby window as I pondered what was going on in Bennet's head. The early afternoon sunshine felt gentle and warm against my skin.

"Sorry I'm late!" Amy called.

Her voice quickly pulled me from my thoughts and grounded me in reality once more.

"It's okay. I haven't been waiting long," I said, pushing a cup towards her as she sat down. "I went ahead and got you your usual."

"Thanks, you're a life saver," she replied, smiling and sitting down.

Amy pulled a small laptop from her bag, placing it on the table and opening it as she spoke. "Here's what I found,"

On the screen were several news articles and detailed weather reports.

"That area Undine mentioned, I'm pretty sure, is Warren Falls," Amy said. "It's a small town about a forty-minute drive away from Clover. They've been experiencing record rainfalls in that area and have been dealing with a weather system for about nine days now."

"That's a lot of rain," I replied, scanning through the various articles on Amy's laptop. "I'm surprised there aren't any mentions of flooding or property damage."

Amy shook her head. "Oh, there is property damage. Undine told you that the rain that came through the area was 'tainted,' right?"

"Yeah," I replied. "It was bad enough that she felt the need to get help from Bennet despite being incredibly vocal about how much she hated humans."

"If that's the case, I think it's safe to assume that this system doesn't act like normal rain," Amy said. "There haven't been any reports of flooding, but there are multiple instances of infrastructure there failing or crumbling, like the very foundation was rotting out. There were even a few bridges and buildings that suddenly suffered from structural failure despite passing inspections less than a week ago. Also, while I've only heard rumors floating around about it online, I've heard a lot of people have gotten sick in Warren Falls."

"Sick?" I parroted back.

"People have been becoming physically weak, apathetic, and even bedridden in some cases," she said. "No one's been able to figure out why."

A look of discomfort subtly contorted itself into her upper lip. "Usually I wouldn't put any stock into rumors like that, but after seeing that Specter and the Otherside firsthand…"

"I get it," I replied. "Given the circumstances, there's a good chance rumors like this are probably more than a coincidence or tall tales."

"Yeah…" Amy said quietly before taking a sip of her Chai Latte.

I felt a little bad for her, knowing about Specters, Others, and the Otherside. It was like peeking behind the curtain. Once you learned that truth, it was almost impossible to go back to the way things were before.

"Were you able to find anything on Emma Thompson?" I asked.

"Sorta," Amy replied. "I wasn't able to find anything about Emma Thompson specifically, but I found a news story in Warren Falls that might be related."

She pulled up a different local news site on her laptop. The next article detailed a car fire caused by an accident involving a drunk driver.

"Only one person died," Amy said. "But that person's name was Noel Thompson. I did some poking around and found out that he grew up in that area, got married a year and a half ago, and that the authorities there had reported his death to his wife, who chose to stay anonymous."

Amy closed her laptop. "This is just a theory, but I think Noel Thompson's wife might be Emma, and his death was the ultimate cause of this somehow."

I felt a bitter taste develop in my mouth at Amy's suggestion.

"A creepy perpetual rain caused by a grieving widow sounds pretty on brand for the misadventures I help Bennet with, unfortunately," I said darkly.

Both Amy and I were sent into a grim silence at this tragic prospect. It was an ugly feeling. Even if you were a bystander who never experienced it firsthand, a thought as emotionally devastating as losing someone dear to you wasn't one you could easily keep at the proverbial arm's length. Even if they were a stranger, watching someone mourn and grieve the loss of someone they love… It's hard not to feel their pain like it's your own. It was an ugly feeling many people go to great lengths to avoid, and that sense of pain hit even harder because I'd experienced that very despair firsthand.

I sighed, attempting to return to my focus on the task at hand.

"Thanks, Amy," I said. "There's no way I could have done research of that quality in such a short amount of time."

"Don't worry about it," she replied. "It's the least I can do after everything you and Bennet have done for me."

"Yuri, you there?" Bennet's voice called.

I caught the faint glow of the charm in my front right pocket with the corner of my eye.

"I need you to get down here as soon as you can."

The light from the charm faded.

"Is something wrong, Yuri?" Amy asked.

"I gotta get down to Warren Falls," I said. "Bennet just called me through his charm. It sounded pretty urgent."

"I'll drive you," Amy said. "It'll take too long if you try to take a bus."

"Thanks," I replied.

#

Amy's car was parked on campus, so we had to walk a while from the coffee shop to get there. We cruised down the state freeway, the grey clouds in the sky above becoming darker and gloomier as we traveled. I sat in the front passenger seat of Amy's sedan, watching cars and greenery pass by and mentally prepping myself for whatever it was that awaited me at our destination.

"Thanks for doing this," I said. "I owe you one."

"Don't worry about it," Amy said, her eyes focused on the road. "I owe you and Bennet a lot. Again, it's the least I can do."

I fidgeted in my seat.

"Hey, Amy…" I said. "Can I talk to you about something?"

"What is it?" Amy asked.

"I've been thinking a lot lately," I said. "About where my life is going, I mean."

Raindrops started to trickle on the car's windshield as Amy drove.

"I only ever started attending Clover because it was the easiest way to get away from my relatives," I said. "I never really ever had a dream, or some bigger goal in my life. I always kind of just faded into the background, thinking it was easier to live a normal life that way. I didn't want any attention from other people, and I didn't want to get close to anyone."

The rain started to pick up as Amy switched on her windshield wipers.

"I learned a while back the full story of how and why my mom died, and I think the last few years, I've been punishing myself for being able to see Specters and eventually believing it was somehow my fault that she..."

I couldn't bring myself to finish that sentence out loud. Instead, I continued.

"My mom's only wish, when everything was said and done, was that I try to live my life without regret. That's why I started thinking about my future and what I wanted to get out of life. And now that I'm doing it, I'm wondering what 'a normal life' even means."

I leaned my head against the window, the glass cold against my skin. "I'm starting to think 'normal' was never in the cards for me," I said. "But aside from that, I don't know where else I'm going. It's honestly a little scary."

Amy pulled off the freeway onto an exit ramp.

"For what it's worth, Yuri," she said. "I think you're pretty incredible."

I practically crawled into my skin upon hearing Amy's compliment; praise was still such an unfamiliar feeling to me.

"Why?" I asked.

"I've only ever gotten a small glimpse of the world you encounter every day," she said. "I'd be lying if I said it didn't scare me. It makes me feel guilty about how overly enthusiastic I got about ghost stories and urban legends when we first met."

"It's not something you have to feel bad about," I replied.

"Still," she said. "I was naive about the whole thing."

Amy smiled weakly. "The fact that you face these things over and over again, and go out of your way to help people like me, I think it's incredible. I could never do it."

I sat up and turned to Amy. "Thanks," I replied awkwardly.

"What I'm trying to say, Yuri, is that it's okay you don't know what you want this very moment," she said. "No matter where you end up, I'm sure you'll land on your feet. Because you're stronger than anyone I know."

I smiled wistfully, recalling how Bennet had said something similar.

"Maybe I'm overthinking things," I said. "Thanks for hearing me out."

The rain was pouring outside as we drove. After a few more minutes on the road, we passed a sign that read "Now Entering Warren Falls." Whatever possibilities awaited my future would have to wait for now, because there was a problem I needed to help solve today. I didn't think I was anywhere near as strong as Bennet and Amy thought I was, but I wanted to at least try to live up to the faith they'd had in me.

CHAPTER 22

RAINDROPS OF SORROW

We pulled into the town square of Warren Falls. Various small independent shops and cafes lined the sidewalks with a small statue of the town's founder in the center. It looked like a place that would normally be filled with people as they peacefully went about their day, but it remained eerie and quiet in the perpetual rain. You could have counted the number of cars we saw driving through here on one hand. I couldn't explain why, but everything about the atmosphere just felt...*wrong*.

"Any idea where we'll find Bennet?" Amy asked.

"He usually tracks me down with the charm he gave me, so he should be close," I explained. "I'd be surprised if he didn't know I was here already."

"Look, there he is," Amy said.

She pointed out towards the sidewalk. Standing by a closed storefront was Bennet, in a baggy emerald green coat, holding a dark maroon umbrella over his head. Amy pulled over and parked the car.

"Wait, before you go," she said, while I unbuckled my seatbelt.

Amy reached into her backseat and pulled out a purple and white checkered pocket umbrella. "Take this. You'll get soaked otherwise."

"Thanks," I replied.

"Stay safe out there, Yuri," Amy said. "Call me whenever you wrap up here. I'll pick you up when you're ready to head back to Clover."

"Will do," I replied.

I got out of Amy's car, opening the pocket umbrella as I stepped out. The only sounds I could hear were the drumming of the rain that fell all around and the hum of the car's engine. Once I reached the sidewalk, Amy waved goodbye one last time from inside her vehicle before driving away, her tires splashing away against the wet road.

It felt unpleasant to be outside right now; that should have gone without saying. The air was cold, and I could already feel the rain soaking through the cuffs of my jeans, but the discomfort went beyond the mere inconvenience of being outside in the rain. It was much more subtle than what I typically experienced, but I could sense the faint aura of dread that lingered in the air. That sense of hopelessness overwhelmed the atmosphere whenever a powerful Specter was nearby.

"You feel it, don't you?" Bennet asked. "This miasma of sadness and self-loathing that chills you to the bone."

I nodded. "Yeah, Something's not right about this place."

I glanced nervously around the town square. "Where is everyone? It's so quiet and creepy."

"Quiet and creepy would be putting it mildly," Bennet replied.

As I looked at Bennet, I realized his skin was much paler than normal. The dark shadows under his eyes were even more pronounced than they were yesterday.

"Are you okay?" I asked.

"I'm fine, Yuri," he said. "Besides, we have more important things to worry about."

Bennet started to walk down the sidewalk with the arm of his umbrella resting on his shoulder, gesturing with his free hand that I should follow.

"How bad is it?" I asked, taking a few brisk steps to catch up.

"It's bad," he said. "The townspeople are starting to feel the effects of this tainted rain as we speak. Most everyone I talked to while I was gathering information was addled with heavy fatigue, short-term memory loss, and lethargy. They're slowly being overwhelmed by the Malevolence that has congealed in the sky. If we don't do anything to cleanse it, this place will be crawling with Specters haunting people."

The wet sidewalk splashed under our feet as we marched onward.

"Once that happens, it'll be just like what Undine said. The local ecology will also start to rot, as life itself here will crumple and wither away. It's like this entire town is experiencing the watered-down effects of an Abscess from the Otherside."

Bennet's eyes glanced up at the ominous dark clouds above us. "Whatever self-loathing invited *this* into the Nearside is truly profound," he said darkly.

I felt my insides tremble and recoil at his words. I could only imagine what Emma must have been going through for something like this to have happened.

"Were you and Amy able to find anything?" Bennet asked.

"Amy did all of the work," I replied. "She couldn't find anything on Emma specifically, but she did find a news story that might be related."

"What did you find?"

"There was a bad car accident before the rainfall started," I explained. "A drunk driver ended up getting into a wreck with someone else. The crash was bad enough that one of the vehicles caught on fire."

"Was everybody okay?" Bennet asked.

"No, the man the drunk driver hit passed away in that blaze," I replied. "His name was Noel Thompson."

Bennet remained silent as we walked.

"Based on what was in the story, Amy and I think that Noel was Emma Thompson's husband."

Bennet abruptly came to a halt. "Shit..." he cursed under his breath.

"You okay?" I asked.

"It's fine, Yuri," he replied with a huff. "It just caught me off guard, is all."

He once again gazed skyward. "I already had a few theories about what caused this surge in Malevolence," he said. "Thanks to Amy's research, I have a very clear picture of what we're up against now. I'm certain what we're dealing with is a Wraith."

Bennet scowled. "A Wraith is kind of like a ghost," he explained somberly. "They're regrets that are left behind in this world after somebody dies."

The raindrops continued to spatter as Bennet spoke.

"Usually, those regrets eventually fade away into nothing, or at worst, end up as a Ghoul stranded in the Collector's domain, but when that despair finds a living person who was deeply attached to the deceased they originated from, they will latch onto them and become a Wraith."

"It's like they're being haunted by an actual ghost," I thought aloud.

Bennet nodded. "Wraiths haunt the bereaved and feed on their grief. The victim's turmoil gives the Wraith form, and it feeds upon that agony and sorrow while stoking even more," he said. "The only times I've seen Wraiths this powerful were when something like survivor's guilt was involved. I can't say for sure why she feels this way, but I believe Emma blames herself for what happened—that somehow, Noel's death is her fault."

Bennet sighed, exasperated. "This job's going to be a rough one," he groaned.

I felt my fingers tighten around my umbrella's handle in response to Bennet's explanation. The pain of losing someone you love. Blaming yourself for their death. It once again hit too close to home.

"We have to help her," I said.

Bennet flashed me a weak smirk. "What do you think we're here to do, dummy?" he replied playfully. "Come on, let's get going."

#

Bennet led the way for about the length of a few city blocks, then we turned down the sidewalk and continued through the residential development built by the Warren Falls Town Square. He stopped when we arrived at a white house behind a black fence made of cast iron bars. The clouds above the house were even darker and more foreboding than those at the town square.

The feeling of overwhelming dread was now in full effect. A powerful Specter was nearby. There was no denying it was here.

"This is Emma's home," Bennet said. "I talked to some of her neighbors earlier. They said she hadn't left in a few days. I didn't want to speak with her directly until we got a better idea of what we were dealing with."

Rain splattered and spluttered against the sidewalk.

"She is probably terrified of facing the outside world right now," I said. "I wanted to find a hole to crawl in and never come out when my mom died."

I placed my hand on the fence.

"Why did you kill me, Emma?" a man's voice billowed from the clouds above.

I fell backward, startled by the ominous voice.

"Why, Emma? Why did you kill me?"

The words carried like the wind.

"You heard that too, right?" I exclaimed in a nervous daze, "That wasn't just some Resonance bullshit just now—that was an actual voice, right?"

"That's the Wraith," Bennet said. "Doesn't exactly paint a pretty picture, does it?"

He helped me to my feet, the back of my pants feeling damp after landing on the wet ground.

"We need to do something," I urged.

Bennet gazed upwards at the dark clouds that circled above Emma's home once more. "I'll see what I can do to handle the Wraith directly," he said. "You should go talk to Emma. Even if we can only find a way to ease her pain just a little bit, we might be able to weaken the Wraith and mitigate some of the effects of this rain."

"You're okay with me talking to Emma alone?" I asked.

Bennet sheepishly looked away. "You're much better suited to talk to her than I will be," he said reluctantly. "Besides, someone has to make sure that Wraith doesn't try to interfere."

"Okay," I replied. "I won't let you down."

#

As I entered through the front gate and marched up the front walk, Bennet disappeared into the hazy mist that had started to form. I closed my umbrella as I stepped onto the front stoop. I clapped my hands to my face to try and psych myself up for the task ahead, rogue droplets of water splashing off my coat sleeves. Taking a quick breath to calm my nerves, I rang the doorbell.

After a few moments, I heard the faint sound of footsteps, but no one answered. I rang the doorbell once more. Once again, after a moment of silence, no one answered. I knocked on the door with the back of my knuckle.

"Hello," I called. "Is anyone home?"

I heard more faint footsteps from behind the door. This time, I the lock clicked, and the door cracked open slightly, a chained latch holding it in place.

"What do you want?" a woman's voice called back curtly.

"Are you Emma?" I asked. "Emma Thompson?"

"Yes," she replied. "Who are you?"

"My name's Yuri," I replied. "I wanted to talk to you about Noel—"

"Go away!" Emma spat.

Before I even had a chance to respond, she slammed the door in my face.

"Wait! Emma!" I called. "Please! Open up! I just want to help!"

"Leave me alone!" Emma ordered from behind the door.

"I know you don't have any reason to trust me, but please just hear me out!" I pleaded. "I know what you're going through."

"What do you know?" she shouted. "Leave me alone!"

"I lost my mom four years ago!" I exclaimed. "I thought for a long time it was my fault she died. I'm still trying to learn not to blame myself!"

Emma remained silent.

"I understand how awful it feels to lose someone you care about. When I first lost my mom, it felt like my entire world was shattered beyond repair. I know you're hurting more than any words could describe."

Emma once again remained silent.

"Please," I pleaded once more, "I just want to help."

I stood quietly for what felt like an eternity. Emma didn't say anything, and I didn't hear her footsteps move away either. Just as I was about to give up, the lock clicked open once more, and Emma opened the door fully.

Emma looked like she was probably in her mid-thirties. She was wearing a baggy sweatshirt that was slightly wrinkled, and her bright, strawberry red hair was tied in a messy bun on top of her head.

"Fine, you win," Emma said, "Come on inside before I change my mind."

CHAPTER 23

THE WIDOW HAUNTED

BY A WRAITH

The inside of Emma's house was gloomy and dark. She didn't have any lights on, and most of the curtains on the first floor were closed. Several trash bags that were strained from their excessive contents had been thrown by the front door. The eerie quiet was only punctuated by the faint sound of rain from outside.

Emma slowly sauntered away from the entryway and down a nearby hallway. I placed my umbrella against the wall and took off my drenched shoes before I followed after her.

I finally found Emma in a sitting room staring out a back window. Several framed photos that would have normally been displayed on shelves or end tables were now face down on the surfaces they called home. Emma sat in a large armchair that looked out into her backyard, holding a cigarette and a lighter in her hand. Next to her on an end table were a box of cigarettes and a small ashtray.

"Do you mind if I light one?" she asked.

"Not at all," I replied, sitting down on a nearby couch.

Emma lit the cigarette, holding it in her hand and letting the smoke billow and dance around her.

"Aren't you going to smoke it?" I asked.

"I don't smoke," Emma replied. "They were Noel's... I just like the smell. It's like he's here still with me."

It was like looking into a cracked mirror and seeing my past self in the reflection. I didn't know what to say. Should I have asked about Noel? Should I have asked how she was doing? It felt like any possible thing I could have said or done would have made the situation worse. Thankfully, Emma was the one to break the silence between us.

"How did you know about me and Noel?" she asked. "Did you know him?"

"No," I said. "I just saw that accident in the news. The rest—well, if I told you, you wouldn't believe me." I looked down at my feet, painfully aware of how I must have sounded. "Sorry, I know that sounds creepy and cryptic, but believe me when I say I just want to help you."

"You're a weird kid, Yuri." Emma scoffed. "But it doesn't matter to me. Nothing does now."

She stared out the window into her backyard. The window looked out upon a garden full of sunflowers. They stood tall but were wilted, probably because of the cursed rain that haunted this place.

"Have you ever been in love, Yuri?" Emma asked.

"No," I replied.

Emma gave me a sad and nostalgic smile as she spoke. "I don't think I could ever describe the feeling very well, but it was wonderful. Noel called me his sunflower. He said it was because I stood tall, bright, and proud."

She laughed weakly.

"It was painfully cheesy, like something out of a bad rom-com.
I didn't hate it, though. Whenever he called me his sunflower, he said it so honestly. Sunflowers are my favorite flowers now."

Emma's eyes twinkled as she reminisced about Noel.

"When Noel told me I was pretty, I felt like I was on top of the world. We met when we were in high school, and he always knew exactly what to say to make me laugh or cheer me up when I was down."

Emma took the cigarette in her hand and ground it into the ashtray, putting it out almost instantly with the violent intensity of her sudden motion.

"And now he's gone."

I watched as Emma continued to grind the cigarette, crumpling it in the ashtray, still staring out the window.

"When was the last time you left your house?" I asked.

"Not since I found out Noel died," Emma said. "This place is gonna be my tomb."

I grimaced at Emma's usage of the word "tomb."

"What would Noel say if he saw you torturing yourself, like this?" I asked.

"That I deserve this, obviously," she replied. "It's my fault he's dead. I'm the one who killed him."

"Didn't he die in a car accident?" I asked. "I read about it in a local newspaper article."

. Emma hunched over, tilting her head. "And how did he get into that accident, I wonder?"

Slouching in her chair, she dropped her cigarette into the ashtray. "Before Noel died, we got into a stupid fight," she said. "He stormed off, and later that night—well, you know the rest."

Emma wiped her eyes as she started to tear up. "I can still see and hear him in my dreams. He asks me why I killed him, and I replay that stupid fight over and over in my head. It's like he's haunting me."

She sighed, slumping on the arm of the chair. "You're sweet for worrying about a stranger like me, Yuri. But you're better off showing that kindness to someone else. I'm the reason Noel is dead, and I will rot here as my punishment."

Emma closed her eyes. "I won't make you leave," she said. "But don't waste your time on me. I'm beyond saving. And I'm tired... This stupid rain always makes me feel sleepy. I'm sorry. I need to rest for a while."

She nodded off almost immediately after she said her piece. Emma looked peaceful in her slumber, her chest slowly rising and falling with her breaths. It was a stark contrast to the outright nihilistic depression she'd been burdened with just moments prior.

It bothered me. Was this what Noel would have wanted? Would the man Emma just described to me want her to die, even if the parting ones to each other had been a nasty fight?

I wandered over to the nearby table where several framed photos were placed facedown. I could only assume that whatever the contents were, they had become too painful for Emma to look at. Couldn't say I blamed her. There were times when just thinking about my mom's face still made my heart ache.

I grabbed one of the picture frames and flipped it up. Staring back was a photo of Emma in a wedding dress, her arms locked with a man with short auburn hair and hazel eyes. The joy they radiated was mesmerizing.

I closed my eyes, and in my mind a vision played out. Emma and Noel stood at the altar, exchanging their vows, their voices choking slightly as they held back tears of joy. They cut the cake at their wedding reception, the loved ones cheering as Emma playfully smeared frosting across Noel's cheek. The scene was enveloped in warm sunshine.

"In sickness and in health," Emma's voice said in an echo.

When the light cleared, it gave way to a new scene in the couple's home. Moving boxes were scattered in their sitting room, some of which were half-emptied. Noel sat on a couch, holding an icepack on his lower back. Emma came carrying a bottle of water and a tablet of ibuprofen.

"I told you you didn't have to carry me across the threshold," she said playfully as she handed the anti-inflammatory and water to Noel.

"But it always looked so fun and easy in the movies," he mused.

"It's a movie," she said wryly, "It's supposed to look fun and easy."

He winced as he adjusted himself, swallowing the pain medicine with water.

"I'm sorry," Noel said. "It all just feels like a dream. We bought a house together, and we're gonna start a family together someday. I just want my sunflower to feel as happy as I do."

Emma leaned forward, kissing him on the cheek.

"I already am," she said.

The memory faded into a warm glow of light.

"In good times and bad," Noel's voice echoed.

Noel leaned over a windowsill with a lit cigarette in his mouth, the smoke floating and dispersing outside as twilight gave way to nightfall. Weariness weighed down on his shoulders, fatigue painfully clear in his eyes.

"Noel, what are you doing?" Emma called angrily.

He took the cigarette out of his mouth, exhaling smoke as he put the it out in an ashtray on the windowsill.

"I'm sorry, I didn't hear you come in," he said.

"Smoking kills," Emma said with a saddened look of concern.

"I thought you already quit."

"I'm sorry." Noel sounded fatigued, his words flat and lethargic. "Things at work have been hectic. One person on our team is retiring, two other people got laid off, and now I'm doing their jobs too. My boss won't let up with the workload."

Emma took a deep breath. "I'm sorry," she said. "I didn't mean to snap like that."

She hugged him, desperately trying to ignore the odor of tobacco that clung to his clothes as they embraced.

"I just hate the idea of living life without you. I want us to grow old and grey together."

Noel smiled weakly. "Okay, you win," he said playfully.

Noel took the lighter and the box of cigarettes from his pocket, tossing them aside on a nearby chair.

"I'll quit for good this time, because I wanna grow old with you too."

Emma smiled back. "Go and wash out your mouth so I can kiss you, okay?"

The scene vanished like mist in moonlight. More memories played through my mind in quick succession. The days passed by as Emma waited for Noel late in the evening every day, and he would come home from work looking more drained each night. Her loneliness washed over me every time she wanted to reach out to Noel, but couldn't bring herself to say her feelings out loud.

Emma sat alone, waiting for the door to open. It was late in the evening, and pouring rain splattered against the windows with the occasional flash of lightning and rumble of thunder. She sat with her arms crossed, anxiously tapping her heel on the ground.
The door opened. Noel shuffled in, hanging his coat and umbrella by the door.

"I'm sorry I'm late," he said. "Just another chaotic, no good, awful day."

Emma scowled. "It's almost 10 in the evening," she said.
"It might be time to look for another job."

Noel's eyes wearily narrowed. "The pay's good," he said. "Besides, I have people on my team counting on me."

Emma looked away. "I count on you to, y'know," she muttered.

She leaned in to kiss Noel but froze midway. Her face contorted in disgust from what she smelled.

"You were smoking again, weren't you?"

He backed away, unable to respond or even look her in the eyes.

"I thought you told me you quit? What the hell!"

"What do you want from me?" Noel shouted. "My boss has a stick stuck up his ass because corporate's not satisfied with our profit reports, and he's taking it out on us! I'm just trying to keep a roof over our heads!"

"Oh, forgive me for not wanting to play third wheel to your job!" Emma spat. "Do I mean nothing to you?"

Noel froze. Lightning flashed and thunder roared off in the distance. Noel threw his hands up in the air.

"I... I can't do this right now," he stammered. "I gotta get out of here."

He rushed to grab his jacket and stormed out the door.

"Noel!" Emma cried.

The sound of a car's ignition starting hummed from outside.

"Noel!" Emma cried again, chasing him out the door.

She watched from the doorstep as the headlights of his car flashed before he backed out and drove away.

"Noel!"

A feeling of unease and panic washed over me as memory after memory played in my mind of Emma frantically calling Noel on her phone and getting sent straight to voicemail.

"Noel, I'm sorry," she said. "I shouldn't have yelled at you like that. I know we can work this out. Please! Come home!"

Emma kept trying to call Noel for a few hours, finally giving up and tossing her phone aside in defeat when his automated voicemail announced that his inbox was full. The memory disappeared in a flash of bright light.

"*Until death do us part,*" Noel's and Emma's voices echoed in unison.

She slept on her couch, the morning sun shining through her windows while last night's leftover rain slowly dripped from the house gutters above. A knock on the front door woke her up from her deep sleep. She rushed to open it, greeted by the sight of a police officer standing on her front stoop.

"Is this the Thompson residence?" he asked.

"Yes," Emma said.

"Are you Emma Thompson?"

"I'm her," she answered quietly.

The officer took off his cap and held it solemnly against his chest. "There was an accident late last night," he said. "A drunk driver hit another motorist, and the accident resulted in a car fire. We've identified the victim as Noel Thompson. I'm afraid his injuries were far too severe... He passed away at the scene."

Emma placed her hand over her mouth as she quietly gasped in frozen horror. The officer elaborated on the accident, but his voice faded out. What washed over me was a state of despair and shock that I had already experienced and understood firsthand. Emma was paralyzed, struggling to process the news as she gave the officer a thousand-yard stare.

"I'm sorry, Emma," Noel's voice echoed. *"How could I have been such an idiot? I love you more than anything. I shouldn't have run away. I shouldn't have lied to you or prioritized some miserable office job over you. I'm sorry!"*

#

I opened my eyes, once again standing in Emma's home. She was still fast asleep in the armchair where I'd left her. Thunder quietly rumbled outside, the sound of rain pouring persistently like an ominous white noise.

I finally understood everything. Noel, in his dying moments, felt a great deal of guilt over neglecting his wife. That regret created a Specter that would come to haunt Emma, her own guilt causing the Specter to mutate further. This resulted in the creation of a Wraith, an image of Noel twisted by Emma's belief that she was the one responsible for his death. The Wraith haunted her dreams and trapped her in perpetual rain to simulate the night Noel died. This reinforced Emma's dark feelings, empowering the Wraith even further.

It was a vicious, never-ending cycle of pain created by guilt and self-loathing. The longer it fed into itself, the more the despair spiraled out of control. It was little wonder that the entire town had fallen victim to it now. But what was I supposed to do about it?

"Why did you kill me, Emma?" a voice echoed, cutting off my train of thought

The voice sounded like Noel, but it felt twisted, distorted even. It had to be the Wraith.

"Why did you kill me?" the Specter asked once more in Noel's voice.

The house started shaking, an aura of dread filling the air and intensifying with each passing rumble. Without opening her eyes, Emma started screaming. It was a blood-curdling shriek that I had only ever heard before in a horror movie.

Bennet's charm started to glow in my Pocket.

"Yuri!" he called through the stone, his voice blurred like radio static. "The Wraith was more powerful than I thou—"

Bennet's voice cut out.

"Bennet!" I called desperately while Emma continued screaming in her sleep. "Bennet! Are you okay!"

"Be care… It's gone berser…"

The light from Bennet's charm faded completely as his voice cut off. I could only brace myself for what was to come while Emma continued to scream.

CHAPTER 24

THE DARKNESS BEFORE

THE DAWN

The rumbling only intensified. The air started to feel stagnant and heavy as the rain outside started pouring even harder. Emma was still screaming. I sprinted to her, her eyes still shut tightly as she sat up in her chair.

"Emma! Wake up!" I called, gently shaking her by the shoulders. "Emma! You have to wake up!"

She stopped screaming, but her eyes remained shut.

"He's here…" she muttered quietly and frantically. "He's here…"

"Who's here?" I asked.

"Noel! I'm sorry!" she screamed.

Emma began to grow cold to my touch. I felt a violent chill race down my spine as a foreboding presence appeared behind me.

I spun around in a flash, ready to guard Emma from whatever it was. What stood before me across the room was an eerie shadow that looked like a humanoid cloud.

"It's your fault I'm dead!" the Wraith screeched.

It spoke in Noel's voice, but it was twisted and distorted—a far cry from the loving tone I had heard in Emma's memories.

"I'm so sorry, Noel!" Emma cried.

"Sorry isn't good enough!" the Wraith roared. "If it weren't for you, I'd still be alive! You want to make it up to me? Curl up and die!"

I fought to keep my breath steady as I tightly held Emma's hand.

"Emma!" I shouted. "Noel would never want you to torture yourself like this!"

"It's her fault I'm dead!" the Wraith screeched. "She deserves to writhe in agony for the rest of her miserable life!"

"I'm sorry… I'm sorry..." Emma muttered over and over again.

"Emma!" I called. "You know that Noel would have never wanted this for you! He'd never want you to blame yourself! He wouldn't want you to suffer or to die!"

"She took me for granted," the wraith echoed. "She is an ungrateful bitch."

"Noel…" she muttered, tears streaming down her cheeks.

"Emma!" I called. "You have to listen to me!"

The house rumbled even more violently as the little light that remained inside started to dissipate entirely.

"What you're seeing isn't Noel!" I shouted. "It's a phantom created by your guilt!"

Emma started screaming once more, her body shaking in terror.

"Please, Emma!" I shouted. "Think back to the man you loved! The man you told me about! Even during your worst moments together, did he ever once wish for you to suffer? Did he ever once want to hurt you?"

"It's your fault!" the Wraith screeched.

"He called you his sunflower!" I shouted. "He was happy to be with you! He dreamed of spending the rest of his life with you! He said so himself: he wanted you to be as happy as he was!"

Emma gritted her teeth as she trembled, straining herself to contain her screams.

"In his final moments, the one thing he regretted more than anything was neglecting you! You were his entire world! You're what made his life worth living!"

"You are the reason I'm dead!" the Wraith echoed.

"So, who are you going to believe, Emma?" I declared. "A phantom warped by your guilt and grief? Or the memory of the man you loved?"

A small and warm smile cracked on Emma's face, her eyes still shut.

"Whenever Noel called me 'sunflower,' it made me feel like I was on cloud nine," she said.

"*Emma!*" the Wraith roared.

"I'm sorry, Noel," she said. "I loved you so much. I will always love you. You meant the world to me, too. You were also my reason for living."

The Wraith screamed.

"And because of that, I will always remember you as the man who loved me more than anything."

A warm yellow glow appeared from behind my shoulder as the Wraith wailed in anguish. In a flash of bright light, the Specter vanished. The overwhelming sense of dread that hung in the air disappeared instantly, along with it. Outside the nearby window, the rain spluttered to a grinding halt. The clouds parted and gave way to the warm orange glow of sunset. The light gently lit up the house as Emma returned to her peaceful slumber. I quietly let go of her hand, letting out a massive sigh of relief.

A few minutes passed. When I was certain the worst had passed, I prepared myself to discreetly and quietly leave when Emma opened her eyes. "Oh, Yuri," she said groggily while letting out a yawn. "You're still here?"

"I'm sorry, I was waiting for the rain to let up a little bit before I left," I explained.

Emma stood up, walking over to the window. "Oh, it looks like it finally stopped raining," she said, mesmerized by the light of the setting sun.

I stepped beside her, taking in the light of the sunset as well.

"It's pretty," Emma thought aloud.

The sunlight glistened against the water that steadily dripped from the gutter above the window and the droplets that lingered on the grass outside. The sky glowed a creamy orange that reminded me of marmalade. It was a warm and peaceful sight, something that I had once thought would forever be lost upon me.

"Yeah," I muttered.

Emma stared longingly out the window, gently pressing the tips of her fingers against the glass.

"I think you were right about Noel," she said with a sigh.

"I don't think he'd want me to stop living my life entirely. It was a stupid fight, and I regret everything that happened, but I'd like to think Noel did too. I'd like to think that if things played out differently, we would have made up the next morning."

Her eyes started to tear up. "I wonder if he thought about me before he passed," she choked. "Life really is unfair sometimes."

"Are you going to be okay?" I asked.

Emma nodded, wiping the dampness out of her eyes. "I will be, I just need some time," she said. "Back when I first got the news, my sister offered to let me stay with her for a while. I should take her up on that offer. I don't want to shoulder this alone anymore."

"I'm glad," I replied. "I don't think Noel would want you to suffer alone either."

Emma clutched her hand to her heart, closing her eyes as she solemnly gathered her thoughts.

I smiled. "I should be going now," I said. "I'm sorry for intruding here for so long."

I returned to the door, picking up my borrowed umbrella from the floor.

"Hey, Yuri," Emma said as I opened her front door. "Thank you. I don't think I would have been able to take the next step forward if you didn't come to visit me today."

I paused at Emma's doorstep.

"You're welcome," I replied, "Please take care, Emma."

#

The air still felt brisk and moist outside as I emerged from Emma's home. You could practically see mud and water oozing out of the neighbors' saturated front lawns. Water dripped down from the leaves of trees and trickled from gutters.

Bennet waited at Emma's gate. He was drenched, soaked completely through his clothes. He looked exhausted; the dark shadows under his eyes combined with his pale skin made him look gaunt like a zombie.

"You really are incredible, Yuri," Bennet said.

"And you look like hell," I replied, marching down Emma's walkway towards the mage. "You good?"

He shrugged. "The Wraith put up a hell of a fight, but it was worth it. It bought you the time you needed to exorcise the damn thing," he said. "How's Emma?"

"After everything that happened, she's still struggling," I said. "But I think she'll be okay."

"And you?"

"It hit close to home, but I'll survive."

"That's good, I—"

Bennet collapsed to the ground mid-sentence.

"Bennet!" I cried. "Are you okay?"

I scrambled to the ground, examining him.

"I'm fine," Bennet replied in a daze, "I used more power than I anticipated. I'm just a little tired, is all."

I scowled, my patience growing thin as I helped Bennet to his feet, prepared to catch him at any moment if he showed signs of losing consciousness again.

"Most people don't pass out because they're 'a little tired!'" I snapped. "Something is wrong! What is it?"

Bennet nodded. "You don't need to worry about it, Yuri," he said. "I have to go now."

In the blink of an eye, Bennet disappeared.

"Bennet, wait!" I called.

I clenched my fists at my sides, just as angry with Bennet as I was worried about him.

"Bennet… You asshole!" I cursed under my breath.

I wanted him to open up to me. Why did he have to disappear like that? It was so frustrating. I wanted to be there for him, but he wouldn't let me. What was I supposed to do?

I took a deep breath, letting my anger ease slightly as I exhaled. There wasn't anything I could do about it now. At the moment, I needed to focus on getting home. Saying that today was exhausting would have been a gross understatement. It was time to get some rest.

#

Amy drove me back from Warren Falls and dropped me off at my apartment. I told her everything that happened with Emma, but I didn't mention Bennet collapsing or my frustration that he'd been so quick to push me away when he was visibly struggling. It was probably hypocritical of me, but I couldn't bring myself to mention it to Amy quite yet. My mind was still a hot mess from it all, and I wanted some time to sort it out myself before I asked for someone else's advice.

Still… I couldn't shake this foreboding feeling that pooled in the pit of my stomach. It was a faint but persistent anxiety that lingered no matter how hard I tried to distract myself.

I was lying in my bed, attempting to read a fantasy novel I had bought over winter break. I glossed over the lines over and over again, unable to concentrate and fully absorb their meaning.

I groaned, dropping the book on my chest in defeat. I was tired, and my thoughts felt like a mess of tangled hot iron scraps. I kept replaying so many different conversations I had with Bennet in my head.

I thought about how Bennet would always wear some seemingly carefree devil-may-care smile, occasionally letting his mask slip when the topic of his past came up. I thought about how he felt so ashamed of a mistake he had made that he couldn't bring himself to speak of it. I thought about how he was always so quick to downplay his own pain with a cocky grin. Bennet was always ready to help others, but he never let anyone return the favor, even when he could barely stand.

I closed my eyes as my mind puzzled over the enigma that was Bennet Grey. My arms and legs felt heavy as my thoughts all started to blur together. Surrendering to the fatigue washing over me, I finally let myself fall asleep.

#

I found myself in a dark void. Bennet stood in the distance. He looked weak, his skin waxy and ghostly pale. His breathing was labored. My feet were firmly planted on the ground, and I couldn't move as I reached out to him.

"Bennet!" I called.

He flashed me a pained smile.

"I'm sorry, Yuri," he said. "I screwed up. I don't have much time left."

Cracks started to form in his face, like he was a statue.

"Bennet!" I called.

"I've long overstayed my welcome in this world," he said.

More cracks appeared over Bennet's face and body.

"I'm sorry, Yuri," he continued, wincing as he bent over and clutched his chest. "I wish I could have stuck around a little longer. It was fun getting to know you, Yuri."

"Bennet! Don't go!" I cried.

His hand trembled as he reached out to me.

"Goodbye… Yuri…".

In an instant, Bennet shattered like glass.

"Bennet!"

CHAPTER 25

GH_ST

I bolted upright in my bed in a panic. A cold sweat dripped down the back of my neck. I took slow breaths as I tried to calm my racing heartbeat. I slowly got out of bed, shuffling to my bathroom. I splashed cold water on my face, desperately trying to pull myself together. It was just a nightmare. There was no point getting worked up about such a thing… right? I'd had plenty of them before, and this one surely wouldn't be the last. But why? Why did that one shake me so badly?

I staggered out of the bathroom, still unsure what to make of my dream. The clock on my microwave read 8:37 AM, and the morning sun lazily peered through my apartment window like it would on any other day. I couldn't shake the image of Bennet shattering like glass in my dream.

"I've long overstayed my welcome in this world."

Bennet's words reverberated in my mind. I couldn't shake this awful feeling that something bad had happened to him. I nervously glanced at the charm on the folding table next to my bed.

My dream, Bennet collapsing after fighting the Wraith that haunted Emma, and then brushing me off so abruptly after the fact—there was no way that combination was a coincidence, right? I hoped that this gut instinct I had was wrong, and that Bennet was back in his house in the Otherside, waiting for me to visit like usual.

A knock on my door reeled me back into reality. I was spiraling so hard, I didn't even realize that it had begun raining outside.

I clapped my hands to my cheeks, desperately trying to pull myself together, before answering the door. Undine stood outside, an umbrella shielding her from the rain that accompanied her.

"Good day, Yuri Weissman," she greeted.

"Hey, Undine," I replied. "Is there something you needed?"

The rain sprite shook her head. "I just wanted to come by to offer my thanks," she said.

"It's no big deal," I said. "I just wanted to help anyway I could."

"I've never known a human to demonstrate such modesty… It's refreshing," Undine mused. "That said, you've impressed me. Loath though I am to admit it, you were able to cleanse a curse that even I was incapable of handling. It's a commendable feat."

"You're too kind," I replied. "Besides, Bennet did most of the heavy lifting. You should make sure to thank him as well."

Undine stared at me quizzically, tilting her head in confusion. "Who's Bennet?" she asked.

I felt myself freeze at Undine's question. I couldn't process it. My brain chewed and chewed on it over again. "Who's Bennet?" No matter how hard the gears turned, I couldn't process the question or why Undine would ask such a thing.

"You're kidding, right?" I finally said. "You came here two days ago asking me to take you to him."

"I don't know what you're talking about," Undine replied.
"I came and asked for your help cleansing the blighted rain brought about by the human known as Emma Thompson. No one else was involved."

I could feel my hands shaking.

"You seriously don't remember?" I asked again. "You're messing with me, right?"

Undine sighed in annoyance. "It seems I've caught you at a bad time," she said. "I've already said my piece, so I'll be on my way then. Farewell, Yuri Weissman."

#

Undine left with a blunt and quick goodbye, taking the rain with her as she departed. I still stood in the doorway, shellshocked by her apparent inability to remember Bennet. Was this like what happened with Bennet's teacher? Was Bennet gone for good?

I didn't think so. I could still remember Bennet clearly, and he had told me that the circumstances that prolonged his life were different from those of his teacher. Bennet was always hesitant to share details about his past, but yesterday, when he was struggling and could barely stand, was the only time he'd ever outright lied to me. I had no idea what was happening, and it terrified me.

Bennet's charm stared at me from the folding table next to my bed. The bright green stone, bound by a leather string, glistened in the sunlight from my window. The sight grounded me, allowing me to compartmentalize my panic for the time being. It was no use wondering and asking questions that couldn't be answered in my apartment right now. I needed to go to the Otherside and make sure Bennet was okay. I took a deep breath, grabbing the charm, and hanging it around my neck. The stone felt cold in my hand as I clutched it to my chest, bracing myself for whatever I would find in Bennet's home.

#

I entered the foyer of Bennet's house using my apartment door.

"Bennet!" I called.

There was no response. I slowly journeyed to the sitting room where he had always awaited my arrival before.

"Bennet, where are you?" I called once more, "Is everything okay?"

The sitting room was empty. The purple couch Bennet often lounged on while smoking a cigarette was also empty. The gentle breeze from the terrace outside only further punctuated the silence caused by his absence.

"Bennet!" I called, my worry growing as I marched to the terrace outside.

Yet again, he didn't answer. The pastel pink cherry blossom petals that fell from the tree that towered above Bennet's house felt disorienting. Desperate, I called for someone else this time.

"Fornax!" I called. "Hey, Fornax! Are you there?"

The pixie flew out from a nearby potted plant. "Yuri-Birdie!" they squealed in excitement. "Is Yuri-Birdie here to play with this one?"

"Maybe later, Fornax," I replied. "I need your help with something."

They fluttered around my head like a butterfly. "What is it, Yuri-Birdie? What can this one do to help Yuri-Birdie?"

"I need your help looking for Bennet," I said. "Have you seen him anywhere?"

Fornax tilted his head like a confused and curious child. "Benn-ET?" they asked, struggling with the syllables.

"You know, the man who lives in this house. You call him 'Bennie.'"

Fornax gave me a stony, baffled stare. All the pixies I'd encountered so far were so hellbent on playtime and games that seeing such a confused and serious expression on one was downright off-putting.

"What is Yuri-Birdie talking about?" they asked. "It's been at least one hundred years since any human has lived in that house."

I felt my heart hit the floor. It was just like before with Undine.

"This one doesn't know who Benn-ET is, but this one hopes Yuri-Birdie finds Benn-ET soon. Benn-ET sounds super important to Yuri-Birdie. Sorry this one could not help."

"It's okay, Fornax," I said. "I have to get going now. I'll play with you the next time I visit."

"Yay!" Fornax cheered. "See you later, Yuri-Birdie! Good luck finding Benn-ET!"

#

I hastily departed from the Otherside after my exchange with Fornax. My body trembled in panic as I stood outside my apartment. First Undine and now Fornax. Something, without a doubt, was very wrong.

"I've long overstayed my welcome in this world."

The words Bennet spoke in my dream haunted me like a ghost. Was I crazy? Had I just imagined him this whole time? What was even happening?

I clenched the charm hanging around my neck. It was the only proof I had that Bennet Grey was a real person who'd saved me from myself. It was the only proof I needed.

I pulled out my phone and made a call. After a few rings, the next person on my list picked up.

"Hello," Amy said through the speaker.

"It's me," I said. "I'm sorry for calling you out of the blue like this, but I need to talk to you in person right away. Can you meet me outside your dorm in twenty minutes?"

"Okay," Amy replied, a hint of confusion in her tone.

"Thanks, I'm heading out now," I said.

I hung up without saying goodbye in my haste. After placing my phone back in my pocket, I rushed to campus, trying not to break into a full-on run.

#

I sat on a bench outside Amy's dorm, tapping my right foot against the ground as I anxiously awaited her. The sun was warm, and the slight breeze was brisk. It was a beautiful spring day in Clover. The nice, calm weather felt jarring compared to my frantic mental state. I anxiously tapped my fingers against my leg, trying to muscle through the pit of anxiety that had pooled in my stomach.

"Sorry about the wait," Amy called as she emerged from her dorm's front entrance, covering her mouth as she let out a small yawn.

"Amy," I said, getting up from the bench. "I need to ask you something."

"What is it?" she replied. "What's so important that we couldn't talk about it over the phone and you had to rush here on a Sunday morning?"

"Amy," I said, my gaze unflinching. "Do you remember someone named Bennet Grey?"

She looked at me in confusion, her eyes wide, clearly startled and perplexed by my urgency.

"What's this abou—"

"Please tell me you remember?" I cried, practically breathless from the suspense of it all.

Amy closed her eyes, lightly tapping the side of her head with her left hand as she tried to recall something.

"No," she said. "I don't remember anyone named Bennet Grey."

CHAPTER 26

THE OBSERVER

It was a fleeting moment that felt like it would never end.

"I don't remember anyone named Bennet Grey," Amy had said.

It didn't feel real. Was Bennet really gone for good? I felt so shell-shocked by Amy's statement that the slightest breeze would have been enough to knock me off my feet.

I stumbled back to the bench I had been waiting on. I could hardly breathe, as once again my mind struggled to process everything that was happening.

"Are you okay?" Amy asked.

"No," I replied with a blank stare.

"What's going on, Yuri?"

"If I told you, you'd think I'm crazy."

Amy sat down next to me. "Any crazier than another world where you saved me from a monster drawn to my repressed feelings?" she mused.

I laughed softly at Amy's joke, my shoulders relaxing a bit. "Fair point," I replied.

I sighed, staring up at the clouds that lazily glided against the bright blue sky above.

"Bennet Grey," I said. "The man I asked if you remembered. Something bad's happened to him, and I don't know what it is.

I saw him in my dream last night, and he said he had long overstayed his welcome in this world. When I woke up this morning, it was like he never existed. No one I've talked to today remembers him, and I haven't been able to find him anywhere."

I gestured to the charm hanging around my neck. "This stone is the only proof I have that he existed," I said. "It's made from crystallized magic, and he gave it to me not long after we first met."

"That sounds scary," Amy said. "You must be worried."

I nodded. "You're absolutely sure you don't remember Bennet?"

"No," she said. "At least, I don't think I do."

"What do you mean by that?" I asked while crossing my arms.

Amy bit her lip. "It's weird. I can't explain it. I don't remember anyone named Bennet, but something also feels off with my memory from when we ended up in that strange world back in September. It's like something's missing," she thought aloud.

I looked down at the ground in defeat. "That's something at least, but it's not much of a lead."

Amy's eyes lit up with a flash of inspiration. "Wait!" she exclaimed. "What about that Observer lady who saved us from the pixies? She said it was her job to watch over everyone and record their lives. Maybe she knows what happened to Bennet."

That suggestion made me remember something very important. Bennet's words rang in my head as clearly as a ringing bell.

"If anything happens to me, I want you to seek out Lucia. Promise me."

I bolted up from the bench. "I gotta get to the Otherside," I said.

Amy nodded. "Be careful, Yuri," she said. "Good luck."

"Thanks, Amy!" I called as I ran off. "I'll talk to you later!"

#

I ran to the Student Center, making my way to the same janitor's closet that Bennet had used to take me to the Otherside for the first time. I closed my eyes and did everything I could to recall the day Amy and I had gotten lost in the Otherside. I pictured the pastel-colored flowers and bright pink sky in my mind as I stroked my fingers down the center of the door. It felt like a long shot, but if I returned to that place, there would have been at least a chance that I'd run into Lucia again.

I knocked on the door with the back of my knuckle.

"I journey to the Otherside," I said.

I opened the door and emerged into the same garden from that day. It was just as I remembered it. A meadow of flowers that looked like it came straight out of the pages of an old children's storybook. As I closed the door behind me, I was greeted by a familiar voice.

"Greetings, Yuri," Lucia said. "I've been expecting you."

She stood before me, the clashing purple and yellows from her dress almost straining my eyes against the warm pastel flowers that bloomed as far as the eye could see.

"How did you know I'd be here?" I asked.

"I'm the Observer. It's my job," she said. "You're here about Bennet Grey. Come." She gently beckoned me to follow her with her hand.

"If you knew I was looking for Bennet, how come you waited for me to come here?" I asked as I walked after her.

"It's simple," Lucia replied. "Because of my station, I have to follow a specific set of rules. Not directly meddling in the affairs of humans and Others is one of them. Unless the natural order of the world is at stake, I am only to watch and record events that take place in the lives of people and Others. I can give those who ask the information they seek, but I am forbidden from telling them what to do with that information. I am to let events unfold unimpeded, without interfering."

"Do you know where Bennet is?" I asked. "Do you know what happened to him?"

"Yes and no."

I bit my cheek in annoyance. "Which is it?"

"It'll be easier for you to understand if you witness with your own eyes," Lucia said.

As we walked, the earth below started to shift and change, molding itself dramatically. Towering bookshelves started to emerge from the flowers, each containing a myriad of tomes that varied wildly in appearance. Some were large and thick, bound in peeling leather, while others were rail-thin paperbacks that looked like they would instantly dissolve when exposed to water.

"Are these books—"

"The records of lives lived," Lucia said. "Many chronicles are ongoing, while others were shelved and archived quite some time ago. Whenever a soul from the Farside is reborn, it is my duty to record the life that it lives and then archive it upon the soul's inevitable return to the Farside."

It was hard for me to take in the majesty of such a sight.

An archive for every life lived, essentially an archive for all humanity and Others.

"Ordinarily, I am forbidden from sharing the contents of these tomes with mortals and Others," Lucia said. "However, between Bennet's request and the unique nature of the current situation, I will have to make an exception."

"What's happening?" I asked. "Is Bennet okay?"

"Once again, it'll be easier to understand if you witness it with your own eyes," Lucia said.

She gently clapped her hands. Suddenly, a patch of earth in front of me raised itself upward and molded itself into a table. In a flurry of flower petals, a tome appeared in Lucia's hands. It was much larger than any of the books I could see on the other shelves. Bound in black leather, the stitching was frayed, the leather peeling around the spine.

"This is the record of the man known as Bennet Grey," Lucia said. "Utilizing your affinity for Resonance, you will be able to witness his life as it unfolded. He asked that, should the worst come to pass, I show you the past he couldn't bear to bring himself to speak of out loud."

She held the tome over the table that had materialized.

"Before we go any further, I must ask: are you prepared, Yuri?" Lucia said slowly. "The memories here contained in this tome are those of profound misery. Once you witness them, there will be no going back. Knowing this, do you still wish to witness this record's contents?"

I glanced at the hefty book in Lucia's hands. My heart was already set.

"I had all but given up on living entirely when Bennet found me. He saved my life," I declared. "If I didn't do everything I could to help him when he needed me, it'd haunt me until the day I die."

Lucia gently nodded. "Very well," she said, placing the book on the table before me.

I set my hand on the book. In an instant, my head felt like it was being stabbed by a knife. Voices echoed and screamed in my mind, the din of them shouting over each other making their words incomprehensible. My vision blurred, and before I knew it, everything went dark as I fell to the ground.

CHAPTER 27

THE ORIGINAL

It was like before, with Spencer's memories—when I plunged into somebody else's heart and witnessed their life play out before my very eyes for the very first time. It felt like I was floating underwater, a torrent of various raw emotions washing over me like a riptide. I could hear Bennet's voice ripple and reverberate all around me.

*"At least **try** to find some reason to keep living!"*

"Do you think I take pleasure in this? I hate that I have to do this, too!"

"You're far stronger than I am, Yuri."

"If anything happens to me, I want you to seek out Lucia."

At last, the feeling of being washed away started to subside.

I felt dwarfed by the silence and nothingness that surrounded me.

"Once upon a time," Lucia's voice echoed from above, *"During a history long forgotten, a man returned from his journey to his beloved."*

In what looked like an old library in an old castle, a woman sat in a chair, reading by sunlight that shone through a wide-open window. Her hair came down in blonde ringlets, and she wore an emerald green dress, like a princess from an old fairytale.

"Agnes, I'm back," a familiar voice called.

A man entered the library. He was not the man that I knew in the present day, but the resemblance was unmistakable. This man would one day become Bennet Gray. His hair was shorter, more well-kept, and his bright blue eyes sparkled in a way that I had never seen. He wore a dark black cloak over a faded grey tunic.

"Welcome back, my love," Agnes greeted, the sound of her voice soft and gentle.

"I'm sorry for being gone for so long," Bennet said. "The Order was tasked with clearing a blight plaguing a distant village. They needed every capable mage to lend a hand."

He knelt down and kissed Agnes's hand.

"It's okay," she said. "I know you were only doing what had to be done. Besides, you were never the type to turn a blind eye to those in need, either." She giggled playfully. "It's one of the reasons I love you."

"You know me too well," Bennet said. "Still, with our wedding so close, nothing will pull me away from you right now." He smiled, gazing lovingly into Agnes's eyes. "I can't wait to spend the rest of my life with you."

"They were deeply in love," Lucia's voice echoed.

The memory started to melt away as the Observer continued. *"The man was engaged to Agnes when they were both children. They became close friends in their early years, and childish affection eventually gave rise to a gentle and passionate love. They were to be married in a few short weeks."*

A new memory began to ooze into creation.

"Their joy would be short-lived, however."

In an old infirmary, Agnes was lying in a bed, deathly pale with a cold sweat dripping down her forehead. Her curls were frizzy, and she breathed weakly. Bennet sat over her, holding her hand tightly.

"Agnes," he said softly. "Please don't leave me."

She smiled weakly, despite the intense pain she felt. "I'm sorry I couldn't stick around longer, my love," she said. "Fate can be quite cruel."

"Agnes…" Bennet choked, his eyes tearing up.

Struggling, she raised her free hand, gently caressing Bennet's cheek. "For what it's worth, my love, you've made me happier than words can say. The moments I've spent with you were the happiest I've ever had. I wouldn't trade them for anything in the world."

"Agnes," Bennet choked once more.

"Please, my love," she said. "Please do not weep for me for long. I want you to keep living. I want you to always know the same happiness that you were kind enough to give me."

Agnes smiled, weakly gripping Bennet's hand in her own and holding it close to her face.

"I love you so much," she said.

Agnes's hand fell back to her bed as she went stiff and silent.

"Agnes…" Bennet choked.

Bennet trembled, standing over Agnes and clenching her limp hand. Tears rolled down his face.

"Anges!"

The sound of Bennet's whaling echoed as the memory melted away. His grief washed over me and chilled me to my bones.

"The man cursed his beloved's fate," Lucia echoed. *"He could not dream of a life without the woman for whom he devoted his everything. Without Agnes, his life was no longer worth living."*

A new memory began to come to life. It formed into a stone-cold room with various tables strewn about, each cluttered with old tomes, peculiar specimens, ingredients, and hand-drawn sigils on parchment. In the center of the room was a table covered in a white cloth where Agnes's body had been placed. Bennet stood over her. His red hair was disheveled, and he had dark shadows under his eyes, his face ghostly from poor sleep and lack of eating.

"The man had sought to cheat death," Lucia said. *"To bring back the woman whom he valued more than life itself."*

There was a series of intricate runes drawn on the floor all across the room. The runes resembled strange symbols and patterns that collectively formed a large circular shape around the table where Agnes's body was laid.

"The man preserved Agnes's body using magic. He sought to research spells that few would even dare to meddle with. In his research, he came across a ritual that could bring someone back from death's cold grasp."

Bennet gently stroked Agnes's cheek, then moved a lock of her hair away from her face.

"The apex of magic is the ability to manifest a miracle. However, to manifest a miracle of such great scale, something of equal value must be offered up in exchange."

Lucia's voice echoed. *"It was one of the basic tenets of magic."*

The runes on the floor started to glow with a bright light.

"The man was prepared to offer up his own life in exchange for that of the woman he loved more than anything. As long as he could see her just one last time, even if it was only for a brief, fleeting moment, then he would make the trade happily and without a second thought."

The runes started to pop and crack, the magic going haywire as it sparked along the drawn lines like rogue lightning. Bennet's eyes frantically darted from one rune to another as the sound began to grow louder and louder. A flash of bright light burst and was accompanied by an explosion. When it cleared, everything but Agnes was blown across the room.

Bennet winced as he got up from the ground after being thrown against one of the walls. Agnes's eyes were open, her breath slight, but otherwise unmistakable. Despite this, she didn't move an inch or even acknowledge Bennet's presence.

"Unfortunately," Lucia echoed, *"the man failed to fully grasp the nature of the forces he tried to tamper with."*

"Agnes," Bennet said, scrambling to the table. "You're back!"

He grabbed her hand. "Agnes, please say something to me!" he pleaded.

Agnes did not respond. Her eyes were open, but no light remained. Her eyes were cold. Hollow.

"You pitiful fool," another familiar voice boomed.

Stepping from the darkness was Peter. Wearing a dark black robe, he almost looked like the spitting image of the Grim Reaper himself.

"You have meddled with forces far beyond your understanding," he said coldly.

"Who are you?" Bennet said, his voice trembling.

Peter slowly edged closer to Bennet, not even addressing his response. "Are you happy?" the Collector said. "To have awakened her in such a pathetic and incomplete state?"

Agnes remained motionless, completely unresponsive to everything going on around her.

"What do you mean?" Bennet barked back.

Peter glared at Agnes. "You have succeeded in resurrecting her flesh, but once a soul reaches the Farside, it cannot ever return to its previous vessel. What you created is an empty husk that can feel no desire or pain. Her body will lie there until it starts to decay."

Peter directed his glare at Bennet. "As for you," he said coldly. "The bargain you were trying to make could never be fully completed to begin with. The price was only half paid. As a result of your foolishness, you are neither dead nor alive. You are now a paradox that blights this world!"

Bennet's face twisted itself into an expression of unbridled rage.

"How dare you! You don't know anything about me or Agnes! Agnes will wake up! She'll—"

In one fluid motion that he performed faster than the blink of an eye, Peter thrust his arm through Bennet's chest and cut off his words, impaling him with one simple thrust. Bennet's eyes bulged in pain as he choked on his blood. I felt my stomach churn violently at the sight, keeping myself from vomiting at the sight by sheer willpower alone.

Peter pulled his arm back in the same fluid motion. Bennet fell to his hands and knees, coughing up blood as he desperately gasped for air. To both my and the past Bennet's horror, the wound that Peter had made stitched itself in seconds. The pools of blood on the floor and the blood stains in Bennet's tunic and cloak were all that remained of the Collector's assault.

"Do you see now?" Peter said as Bennet continued gasping for air.

Bennet trembled, staring at the hole in his tunic and back at Peter.

"You will never age. You will never die," the Collector said. "You will be a phantom forever frozen in time. Eventually, your very soul will wither and rot away long before your body."

Peter then vanished into the darkness. "That is the fate you brought upon yourself," his voice echoed.

The memory melted away.

"The man would spend the centuries to come wandering aimlessly," Lucia's voice echoed. *"He had nowhere to belong, and he desperately awaited a death to release him from his suffering that would never come."*

A profound hopelessness washed over me like torrential rain. It started small and began to grow. One by one, more memories flashed before my eyes. I watched in terror as, over multiple decades, Bennet continued to try to end his life. Stabbing himself, jumping off cliffs, and letting himself be attacked by feral animals. No matter what he attempted, he arose once more without a scratch. Just like the rain, Bennet's pain and suffering were continuous and unrelenting. Inescapable.

Bennet slowly marched through a field alone. He was covered in grime, soil, and dried blood. There was no light in his eyes as he staggered onward. Finally, after taking another step forward, he fell to the ground. His eyes were half open, and his lips were cracked and chapped. It was like he had given up on everything entirely, and he was lying on the ground, waiting for the world itself to end.

"Are you okay?" a male voice called.

A man stood in the distance. I couldn't make out his face or what he looked like. It was like the man himself was a blurry image that could never properly come into focus.

"It was a chance encounter with the Original; the person would eventually become this man's teacher," Lucia's voice echoed. *"The Original was a gentle soul who could not turn a blind eye to those in need."*

In the same house I had visited so many times before in the Otherside, Bennet was slumped on a couch. He sat sullenly in a set of borrowed clothes, his body washed of the physical filth that had accumulated. He stared down at the ground, eyes still devoid of any light or any desire to live. The man who found him sat across from him, still appearing blurry.

"What's your name?" the Original asked.

If nothing else, I could make out the Original's voice clearly.

It was a deep baritone that reminded me of an oak tree. Firm and strong, yet warm and gentle.

"Do you have anywhere to go?" the Original asked.

"No," Bennet replied without lifting his gaze from the ground. "I have no name, and I have no place to call home. The man I was died a long time ago."

"What happened?" the Original asked.

"I made a mistake so awful that I will never know peace from it," Bennet said. "I cannot die. I am a phantom that will wander this world with no place to go for the rest of eternity."

Bennet's was crushed by the weight of his own nihilism. He sat there silently, listlessly, and barely moving.

"If you have no place to go," the Original said. "Why not stay here with me?"

Bennet slowly gazed up at the figure, a shocked expression slowly forming on his face. "But I don't deserve such kindness—"

"I'm giving it anyway," the Original said. "I do not care if you feel like you deserve it. My kindness is mine to give as I see fit."

Tears started dripping down Bennet's face. "Why do such a thing for me? What I have done cannot be forgiven—"

"Then live to atone for it," the Original said. "Live so that one day you may come to forgive yourself."

Bennet's eyes widened.

"Life is too precious a thing to be spent yearning for death," the Original said.

It felt like déjà vu. It was like watching when Bennet first met me. His sadness, the gentle warmth that brought him back from the brink, it was all so familiar to me. I started to tear up alongside the past Bennet before me.

"The Original took this man under his wing and taught him everything he could," Lucia's voice echoed. *"The man would eventually adopt the name of Bennet Grey. Thanks to the Original, he found new purpose, learning everything he could about the Malevolence Phenomenon and Specters, and making it his mission to help preserve the world's balance as an act of reparation and atonement for the mistake he made so long ago."*

Outside the house I knew as Bennet's home, standing at the base of the cherry blossom that towered above, were Bennet and the Original. Behind the latter was a piece of paper neatly folded and hammered into the tree's base.

"I couldn't be any more proud of you," the Original said. "You've grown a lot in the past few years."

Bennet smiled awkwardly. "I had a good teacher," he replied.

Bennet sighed, the smile on his face replaced with a melancholy look. "Are you certain you have to do this?" he said.

I still couldn't make out the Original's face, but when he next spoke, I couldn't help but think he had a content expression because of the brightness in his words.

"I bound my soul to the Otherside long ago," he said. "Everything I've done was because of this world I've come to love so much. I know it's full of unspeakable sadness, sorrow, and despair, but there were many wonderful things I've had the pleasure of experiencing as well."

"You were always the idealistic type," Bennet said.

"Just the musings of a sentimental old man," the Original said. "I taught you everything I know, Bennet."

A gentle wind blew, Bennet's hair billowing slightly in the breeze.

"It's good to respect your elders," the Original said. "But old war horses like me also need to know when it's time to bow out so that new generations may grow and flourish."

"You say that like I'm not also as old as dirt," Bennet said with a playful bite.

The Original placed his hand on Bennet's shoulder. "My time has come," he said. "It is time that I return my soul to the Farside. I leave my work in your capable hands, Bennet."

Bennet smiled, teary-eyed. "I won't let you down," he said, trying to maintain a stiff upper lip. "Thank you… Thank you for everything!"

The Original placed his hand on the paper nailed to the tree.

"Farewell, Bennet," he said. "I hope we can meet again in the next life."

The paper and the Original then vanished in a warm yellow glow.

Chapter 28

THE UNFORTUNATE FATE

THAT AWAITS

Bennet's life continued to play out before my eyes. Lucia narrated as I watched him carry on through the 20th century, taking on various requests, clearing Abscesses, and meeting familiar faces, like Detective Linebeck and Fornax. Each memory played out like a scene in a montage as I felt the overwhelming weight of duty that Bennet shouldered as if it were my own.

I had gotten the sense that Bennet had been through a lot, but the ordeals he faced were beyond my wildest imagination. It frustrated me. Why did Bennet feel the need to shoulder everything on his own? Why couldn't he open up to me or ask for help? The questions were pointless, though. I already knew the answer. It was because of the shame from his past that haunted him to this very day. The shame from a mistake he made long ago, that he still he struggled to bring himself to say out loud.

A new memory formed, recreating the day I met him. Lucia recounted our meeting. I watched as Bennet took me to the Otherside for the first time and divined my fortune. It had barely been a year since I'd first met him, but each memory felt like a lifetime in a sense. There was so much that happened, it felt like time had both slowed to a crawl and flashed in a wicked blur.

After recounting our initial escapades to exorcise the Specter haunting Amy, a new memory was formed. Bennet watched from a distance, out of sight of Amy and me, while we carried on with the spirit photography survey that day before I had caused the Poltergeist haunting her to go berserk.

"It's impolite to stare, you know," Bennet said as he observed us. "If you have something to say, then say it, Hades."

Peter stepped forward, appearing like he had just blinked into existence. "Why did you take that boy on as your apprentice?" he said. "Are you seeking a successor?"

"No, Hades," Bennet replied. "I'm not looking for someone to succeed me."

"Then why—"

"You're already aware of the unique nature of Yuri's soul, right, Hades?" Bennet asked, cutting him off.

"I'm quite aware," Peter replied somberly. "Very few souls have managed to return to the world of the living after making contact with the Farside, and his soul might have made the most profound contact I've ever seen."

Bennet exhaled. "He's been through a lot," the mage said. "Whether it was pure coincidence or a work of fate, who can say? Regardless, that incident has given Yuri a potential for magic that I have never once seen before."

Bennet smiled with melancholy as the wind rustled his hair. "And yet that boon has caused him such sadness and misfortune. Call me a sentimental sap, but I saw someone like that, and all I wanted to do was save him from himself and the powers he was cursed with."

Peter glared coldly at Bennet. "Is that wise?" Peter asked, "Considering your predicament."

"I'm fine, Hades," Bennet dismissed with an annoyed bite to his voice. "And while we're on the topic, I'd appreciate it if you didn't try to scare Yuri off or air out the skeletons in my closet behind my back."

"Bennet..." Peter said. "Your soul is starting to crack and decay. There's only so long a soul can sustain itself without returning to the Farside. While your physical vessel will likely carry on, your soul is a different matter entirely."

A gentle breeze blew through the area, scattering fallen leaves.

"At the rate you're going, you're soul will be destroyed in less than a year if you keep overexerting your power."

I felt my heart sink into my chest. It made me angry. It made me sad. I'm not sure which I hated more: the fact that Bennet kept this from me, or the very nature of the cruel hand he was dealt to begin with.

"I know," Bennet said. "I don't have a lot of time left. I've already committed to teach Yuri, and I fully intend to make the most of every moment I have left."

He looked up at the sky, almost longingly.

"Yuri's like a newborn chick right now. He's feeble. Weak. Utterly defenseless, really. But with my guidance, he'll soar farther than I or my teacher ever could."

The Poltergeist that haunted Amy roared in the distance.

Bennet smirked. "He still has a lot to learn, though," he mused. "My presence is needed elsewhere now. Til next time, Hades."

The memories and Lucia's narration marched on, as I witnessed the events that centered around rescuing Amy and Detective Linebeck's request to subdue

Spencer Rhode play out before my eyes. I watched as Bennet frantically called for me as I had fallen unconscious upon touching and examining the chimera corpse.

"Yuri! Wake up!" he shouted as he held me in his arms, my eyes twitching violently behind my eyelids like I was having a nightmare.

I watched as Bennet put Spencer out of his misery, averting my gaze when he set Spencer's mangled, rotting flesh ablaze.

The memories continued playing in sequence, and I witnessed various conversations with Bennet before he escorted me to the Collector's domain. This time, yet another memory I didn't recognize began to take shape.

Bennet and Lucia stood in the same botanical library where my body was currently lying unconscious.

"Lucia, I have a favor to ask," Bennet said.

His tone was pensive as he spoke, grim in a way I had never heard from him before. Another side he didn't want me to see.

"You wish for me to share your past with him, yes?" Lucia said. "Why not share it with him yourself?"

"You already know why," Bennet said darkly.

She nodded. "Yes. I can see it quite plainly. Your soul is brittle and cracked. It could give away any day now."

"I don't have much time left," he said. "You know as well as I do that a soul can only last for so long before needing to return to the Farside. Even if the flesh cannot die, the soul will slowly rot away, leaving behind an empty husk. I am too far gone. There's nothing that can be done to prevent this fate."

"And you're reluctant to share this with Yuri," Lucia said.

Bennet nodded. "All of this was a product of my foolishness all those years ago," he said. "It's my punishment to suffer, and mine alone. Everything I've done since my teacher named me his successor, I did to atone for that awful crime. I toil away, trying to prevent Malevolence from destroying the very fabric of reality, a destruction I've come to believe is an inevitable fate that my efforts are only capable of delaying. I refuse to burden Yuri with any of this."

"Of course," Lucia replied. "You say this, and yet you're painfully aware that in trying to spare Yuri from pain, you'll only cause him more."

"I get it," Bennet said. "I'm a coward haunted by my mistakes. I'm a terrible person."

"Then why ask me to relay any of this information about you?" the Observer asked. "You could very easily disappear without a trace, and Yuri would never be able to find out what happened."

Bennet crossed his arms, sheepishly turning away from Lucia.

"Because I made a promise to him," he scoffed. "I told him that one day, I'd share every skeleton in my closet I've been hiding from him. I still can't bring myself to say what I've done out loud, and I don't have the luxury of time to build up the courage. Even if something happens to me, I still want to be able to keep that promise."

Lucia nodded in affirmation. "You must really care about Yuri," she said.

"You already know why I decided to take on Yuri as my apprentice," Bennet said. "Of course I care about him."

#

I slowly opened my eyes. I was lying on the ground, Lucia standing above me, offering a hand down to help me up.

"Now you know everything," she said as she pulled me off the ground.

I wasn't sure what to feel after what I'd learned about Bennet. It was so much to take in once. I was saddened by the tragedies he'd endured, horrified by the ease with which he'd accepted the destruction of his soul, angry that he kept all of this from me, and all too familiar with the feelings of self-loathing he couldn't let go of.

"So is Bennet...gone?" I asked, choking on the sentence as I forced myself to say the possibility out loud.

Lucia shook her head. "His soul remains, but it's weak. It could shatter at any moment," she said. "In its current state, even I would struggle to track down Bennet's whereabouts. As his soul slowly fades, reality corrects its narrative so that Bennet died those many years ago when he attempted to resurrect Agnes. As a result, almost everyone he's encountered after that point will soon forget that he ever existed. Only those who have a deep emotional attachment to him will have any memory of him."

"How do we save him?" I asked.

"You can't," Lucia said bluntly. "There is no way to repair a soul without returning it to the Farside, and his body cannot die. The burden of his sin and guilt binds him to this world. What will become of his vessel once his soul dissipates, even I cannot say."

I stared in disbelief, crushed by the heavy reality of Lucia's words. It felt so unfair, so utterly cruel, that this was the way things had to play out. Why…why did it have to be like this? Everything about it was so goddamn unfair!

In a sudden burst of light, a wisp appeared. I fell backward, startled by its sudden appearance.

"Luci…it…bad," Peter's voice called through the wisp, his words cutting in and out. "No! Ben…stop!"

Peter screamed in agony as his voice was immediately cut off. The wisp quivered and trembled, flicking its light dimly as it gave a timid chime. Lucia's stony stare was just as deadly serious as it was darkly grim.

"We must go to the Collector's domain right away," she said.

CHAPTER 29

THE MAN HAUNTED

BY HIS PAST

"We have to go to the Collector's Domain right now," Lucia said."I don't have time to explain."

She made several dramatic flourishes with her hands, the earth molding itself as she conducted it. Emerging from the ground was a Travel Glass, like the one from Bennet's house, brightly polished as if it was freshly crafted. Lucia darted over and fogged the glass with her breath before smudging "the Collector's domain" in the condensation. The Travel Glass's reflection warped and contorted before revealing an entryway to the strange world Peter resided in.

"Come, Yuri. We've no time to waste," Lucia said.

Nodding my head, I darted through the Travel Glass, chasing after her.

When we emerged, the air grew heavy in an instant. An aura of dread pervaded the atmosphere so intensely that it made the foreboding presence of a Specter feel like child's play in comparison. It sent a shiver down my spine and made the hairs on the back of my neck stand on end.

I covered my mouth and gasped in horror at the sight before me.

Peter was lying face down on the ground, his body beaten bloody, and the crystals all around him splintered and cracked. Standing above him, with a foot pressed into his back, was Bennet.

Peter weakly raised his head, reaching out his hand towards me. "Yuri...run…" he croaked, trembling.

"Quiet, you!" Bennet barked, stomping Peter's head back into the ground.

It was all wrong. It looked like Bennet. It sounded like Bennet. But the man grinding his heel into the back of Peter's skull felt like another person entirely. Lucia stared blankly, her arms dangling at her sides.

"I have never seen anything like this." She quietly quivered. "His soul is barely holding on, but this rancor, his despair—it's like he's becoming a living Specter."

"Who are you? You're not Bennet!" I shouted.

The man with Bennet's face picked up Peter by his shirt collar.

"Come on, Yuri," he said. "I *am* Bennet. In a sense, at least."

He tossed Peter aside like a rag doll.

"I am Bennet's rage and despair made manifest, the despair he denied for so long," the shade said. "As his soul slowly crumbles away, I get to be the one to call the shots in this godforsaken body."

The shade raised Bennet's arms like a grandiose showman. "I've grown tired of this crappy existence," it exclaimed. "We live to suffer, die, rot away, and get reborn to repeat the same bullshit over and over again. All the while, Malevolence brought on by humanity's collective despair tears apart reality. That despair creates Specters to torment humans, and it creates the Abscesses that corrode the very fabric of reality. Even with Bennet toiling away to repair it, reality and all life as we know it, sooner or later, will come to an end, brought on by humanity's collective despair."

The shade contorted Bennet's face into a wicked, maniacal grin.

"So I thought, 'To hell with it all! If we're all headed for an inevitable doom anyway, let's just skip right on to the grand finale! I'll put an end to this idiotic cycle of death and rebirth and put us all out of our misery!' Easy peasy!" the shade cheered.

I clenched my fists, practically shaking in anger. "Bennet, if you're still in there, I'm going to get you back! Don't you dare give up on me!" I ordered.

"Yuri! Don't!" Lucia cried. "It's too dangerous!"

"Get out of here while you still can, Yuri…" Peter urged, barely clinging to consciousness.

"You should listen to them, Yuri," the shade said. "I'm not like your sappy teacher. I'll tear you to shreds without a second thought."

I raised my arms, readying myself for whatever the shade would attempt.

"I don't care if it's impossible!" I said. "Bennet told me the apex of magic was to bring about a miracle! He believed in me, and I'm sure as shit not giving up now!"

The shade contorted Bennet's face into an ugly glare, eyes cold and ready to kill.

"Stop looking at me with that stupid face of yours!" the shade growled, "The hope in your eyes is revolting! It's pissing me off!"

The shade raised Bennet's arms, dark black magic crackling in Bennet's hands like lightning. "I will show you the one and only truth! The truth known as despair!" the shade roared.

I quickly crossed my own arms, creating a barrier of warm light in front of me, blocking the beam of dark magic the shade launched at me. I dug my heels into the ground, gritting my teeth, bracing my entire body against the sheer force of the attack.

"I'm doing you a kindness!" the shade roared. "To live is to suffer! I'm putting you out of your misery! This is a mercy!"

"Damn it, Bennet!" I shouted. "You don't have to do everything on your own!"

"Just die already!" the shade screamed.

The magical barrage intensified, the force making my knees buckle as I tried even harder to stand my ground.

"Don't you see you're hurting yourself and everyone around you, punishing yourself like this?!" I shouted.

The raw dark magic sparked and surged.

"Shut up!!" the shade roared.

"I'm not giving up on you, Bennet!" I screamed.

My heels ground into the crystals beneath me as I dug them even deeper.

"What would Agnes say if she saw you like this?"

"Enough! Just shut up and die!" the shade screeched.

"Don't you remember her final request?!" I shouted. "That she wanted you to be happy! Did that mean nothing to you?"

The bright light from my barrier intensified.

"Bennet, if you're still in there…it's time to face your past once and for all!"

The shade screeched as the light blinded my eyes. The magical assault I endured weakened before stopping entirely.

#

When the light cleared, I stood in a barren field with sepia-toned clouds brooding above in the sky. Off in the distance, I could see Bennet stagger towards me. He was covered in mud, grime, and dried blood. He had no light in his eyes. As he approached me, Bennet fell forward to the ground, landing on his side as his legs gave out from under him.

"What was this all for?" he sobbed. "Why do we live only to suffer? What is the point of all this hellish misery? What was it all for?"

He trembled.

"Has everything I've done all been for nothing?"

I gave Bennet a gentle smile as I knelt beside him, brushing his messy red hair out of his face, his eyes staring at me like a pair of pale blue moons.

"It's okay," I said. "You don't have to shoulder everything alone anymore."

#

The barren field vanished in the blink of an eye, and I now knelt beside Bennet in the Collector's domain. The tears that were dripping down his face were illuminated by the cool blue light of the crystal all around us. Bennet smiled weakly as he laid on the ground and looked into my eyes.

"Thank you," he said.

In a warm yellow glow, Bennet disappeared like scattering fireflies.

Lucia supported Peter as he limped over to me.

"Yuri," the Collector stammered. "You achieved something impossible. I will forever be in your debt."

"It's alright," I said weakly, the strain on my body finally catching up to me. "I was just helping a friend…"

I collapsed on the floor, too tired to even sit up straight. The weight of my limbs and torso felt like lead. My vision slowly darkened as Peter called my name over and over again. Eventually, everything went black, and I could no longer hear the sound of Peter's voice at all.

CHAPTER 30

YURI'S ANSWER

I opened my eyes. I was on a bench under a cherry blossom tree. A wide-open field stretched as far as the eye could see, the blades of grass dancing and swaying with the gentle breeze. Bennet sat next to me.

"Where are we?" I asked.

"It's a dream," Bennet said. "You passed out after everything that happened in the Collector's domain. Lucia and Peter brought you to your apartment, and you're currently asleep in your bed."

I felt the gentle breeze that blew against my face as the wind whistled off into the distance.

"This is it, right?" I asked. "This is goodbye?"

"Yes," Bennet said. "I wanted to talk to you one last time before I departed this world."

He exhaled.

"I'm sorry for keeping you in the dark about everything the way I did.".

"It's okay, really," I replied. "If I were in your shoes, I probably would have done the same thing."

I bit my lip.

"Hey Bennet," I said. "When you offered to teach me about Specters and asked me to be your apprentice, you're sure it wasn't cause you wanted me to be your successor? Like you did with your teacher?"

"No," Bennet replied.

"Was it because you pitied me?" I asked.

He shook his head. "No, that's not why either."

"Then why did you decide to take me on as a student?" I asked.

Bennet gazed upward at the sky.

"It's cause I saw you as a kindred spirit," he said. "Someone who was torturing themselves that I could potentially save, like my teacher saved me. You reached out to me when you had nowhere else to go. How could I ever turn away someone like that?"

A stray cherry blossom petal drifted from the boughs above us.

"I owe you a lot," I said.

"Consider the feeling mutual," Bennet said. "I was on a path to destruction because I couldn't face my past and make peace with everything I lost. That guilt bound me to this world. I was consumed by pain and misery, and I almost destroyed everything because of it."

Bennet grinned, playfully ruffling my hair.

"But then you rushed in anyway, ignoring all the warnings Lucia and Peter gave, and you defied a fate we all believed was set in stone," he said. "You really are incredible."

I cracked an embarrassed smile.

"I don't know if I'm incredible or not," I replied. "But you believed in me, and I wanted to live up to that."

"You've surpassed my wildest expectations, Yuri," Bennet said. "As your teacher, I couldn't be any prouder of you."

I looked up the boughs of the cherry blossom tree above, watching the petals sway in the breeze.

"Would you want me to succeed you?" I asked.

Bennet shook his head.

"That's completely up to you, Yuri," he replied. "You shape your own destiny. The only thing I ask of you is that you live a life you can be proud of, so when your time comes, you have few regrets to leave behind."

"Okay," I replied. "I will."

The breeze picked up, howling with its gusts.

"For what it's worth, Yuri," Bennet said. "Even with all the ups and downs, I'm really glad I got to meet you. I hope we can meet again in my next life."

The petals from the cherry blossom started to scatter in the wind.

"I'd like that too," I replied.

He patted my shoulder.

"Thank you for everything, Yuri," Bennet said. "Farewell."

#

I sat up in my bed. My arms and legs felt heavy, and I could feel dampness under my eyes, like I had been crying in my sleep.

I could hear the gentle song of a lone blue jay outside, the morning sun shining through my apartment window as I came to. I turned to my nightstand, where Bennet's charm glistened in the sunlight like jade or malachite. I picked up the stone, clenching it in both my hands as I sat up in my bed.

"Thank you," I said.

Tears dripped down from my eyes and onto the stone in my hands.

"Thank you for everything… Goodbye, Bennet…"

I wept for my departed teacher and friend. I sobbed for what felt like hours, knowing full well that I would eventually have to pick myself up from my sadness, because Bennet wouldn't want me to mourn him forever.

April passed without incident, and by the middle of May, my semester had come to an end. It felt like it all passed in a blur.

I cherished every single moment of it. For the first time, I had gotten straight A's on my exams. I made a point to spend as much time as I could with Amy during the remainder of that semester, the first friend my age I ever made. I would always cherish that friendship, no matter what.

Amy and I stood outside my apartment, the sun hot as it beat down on the open terrace.

"I guess it's already time," she said.

"Yeah," I replied. "I'm sorry for doing this."

Amy shook her head. "Don't be," she said. "You're being true to yourself with what you want. It's a good thing."

"Thank you for that, Amy," I said.

Her eyes started tearing up. "Damn it," she cursed, wiping them away with her hand. "I promised myself I wouldn't cry."

I turned around to face my apartment door. I stroked the back of my fingers down the center before knocking twice with the back of my knuckle.

"I journey to the Otherside," I said.

I cracked open the door, revealing the foyer of Bennet's house.

"This is it," I said. "Thanks for sticking with me despite all the craziness. I'm really glad I got to meet you."

I stepped into the threshold of Bennet's house.

"Goodbye," I said.

Amy gave me a warm and pained smile as the tears continued to stream.

"See you," she chimed.

I closed the door behind me, trying not to picture Amy crying after I did.

#

I ventured to the sitting area where I'd sat and talked with Bennet so many times before. It still felt so strange that he was gone now. I brushed my fingers on the couch he used to sit on, savoring the faint, lingering scent of his cigarettes. I gazed down at the coffee table, where I had placed a piece of parchment, a ballpoint pen, some nails, and a hammer. I knelt beside the table, neatly writing "Yuri Weissman" across the paper. After taking a moment to let the ink dry, I folded the paper into a tight square and carried it outside with me, along with the hammer and nails.

I approached the base of the giant cherry blossom tree that towered over the property. Peter was standing nearby, his wounds from the events of late March mostly healed.

"Are you certain you want to go through with this?" Peter asked.

"I am," I replied.

"How did you even come to learn about this ceremony?" he asked.

"I asked Lucia," I explained. "She didn't seem thrilled I was asking about it, but she didn't try to stop me either. That's the Observer for you."

Peter straightened his glasses. "Once you go through with this, Yuri, there will be no going back," Peter said. "You can still turn around and live a normal life if you so desire."

"You and I both know that 'normal' was never in the cards for me," I scoffed while I pressed the paper against the tree's trunk and prepared a nail.

"Are you doing this simply to honor Bennet's legacy?" Peter asked.

"Partially," I replied.

I hammered the nail into the piece of paper, the banging echoing loudly off into the distance. I set the hammer and spare nails down on the ground after I made sure the paper was secure.

"But this is for me too. Bennet was there for me when I was about ready to give up on everything. He saved me."

I returned my gaze to Peter.

"I want to save someone the same way I was saved. I want to be there for someone else when they need it most."

I placed my hand against the tree.

"Besides," I said. "This is something only I can do. I'm okay with the sacrifice I'm about to make. This is what I want."

Peter frowned. "Okay," he said. "As long as you're sure…"

I placed my hand against the piece of paper.

"I, Yuri Weissman, accept this fate of my own free will," I said.

The paper gave off a warm yellow glow.

"On this day, I offer up my name and legacy as tribute to be one with the Otherside. To be unknown in life. To be unknown in death. That is the price I pay so that I may fulfill my duties."

The yellow glow enveloped me.

"From this day forward, I offer up my name and place in history. I choose this fate of my own free will."

The glow faded. A gentle breeze started to blow, signaling the winds of change.

"It's official," Peter said. "You are officially the owner of this domain. There is no going back now."

I turned to the Collector.

"It'll be a pleasure to work with you, Hades," I teased.

Peter let out an amused and exasperated laugh.

"Not gonna let that nickname die, are you?" he said.

"Someone has to keep the tradition going," I said, with a playful, smug grin.

I took in the sights all around me. This was going to be my home for the rest of my life. I knew that it would be a long, challenging path fraught with heartache. I knew that despite everything I would do, there was nothing I could do to fully stop despair from ending all life as we know it one day. Even then, I gladly accepted the challenge. Nothing worth doing is easy.

"Mom. Dad. Bennet. If you guys are watching, I want you to know I'll be okay." I whispered quietly, my words carried by the wind. "This is what I was meant for. So please, rest easy knowing I'm doing something with my life that I can be proud of."

I slumped back against the tree behind me, sliding down against it to sit on the grass below. I clutched the charm I hung around my neck as a memento. I didn't know if I would ever be the incredible mage Bennet thought I was, but nothing would have made me happier than to live up to the expectation of the person who believed in me when I needed it most.

"I accept this wonderful and insurmountable challenge of my own free will."

EPILOGUE

AND SO WE CARRY ON

"Order for Amy!"

"Thanks," I said as the barista handed me my order.

I sat down at an empty table, plopping my laptop bag under my chair. I hadn't been to this coffeeshop in years. Twelve years after graduating, I was asked to speak at Clover College to talk about writing and publishing a novel. My debut work, *The Monsters That Go Unseen*, wasn't exactly a resounding success, but it was still performing way better than I thought it would. Still a bummer that only four people showed up to my lecture, though. An Iced Mocha from my favorite coffee shop as an undergrad was supposed to be a pick-me-up.

I looked out the windows of the coffee shop, staring at the autumn leaves that billowed in the nearby trees. The orange canopies were dazzling in the afternoon sunlight. I swished the iced coffee in my disposable cup. Twelve years later, I was back on campus and not doing as great as I thought I would be by now. It sucked, but that was life.

"Um, excuse me," a voice called.

Standing next to my table was a 20-something college boy with silky black hair and an unzipped charcoal windbreaker, holding a book in one of his hands. He had bright green eyes that sparkled like emeralds, and wore a strange-looking stone tied with a leather string around his neck.

"You're Amy LeBlanc, right?" he asked.

"Yep," I replied.

My eyes widened as I saw that the book he carried was *The Monsters That Go Unseen*.

"You like my book?" I asked.

"A lot," he replied. "I was wondering if you'd sign it for me."

I could feel my entire day turning around.

"Sure, let me see if I have a pen," I said.

I pulled out my laptop bag from under my chair, rummaging through the side pockets for a pen.

"What's your major?" I asked. "I just gave a guest lecture over at the English building."

"I'm not a student here," the boy replied. "I had a job nearby that I finished not long ago."

I finally pulled a pen out of my bag.

"What do you do?" I asked.

"Eh, I won't bore you with the details," the boy said. "They'd just, well…bore you."

"Fair enough," I said as I opened up his book's cover.

"If you don't mind me asking, I was wondering what the inspiration for your main character in *The Monsters Unseen* was?" he asked.

I set the pen down on the table.

"Promise not to laugh," I said.

"Promise."

I stared back outside as I was overcome by a wave of nostalgia.

"There was a boy I knew a long time ago," I said. "Honestly, I can't remember his name or what he looked like. Sometimes I wonder if he was just someone I dreamt up one day."

I rolled my pen between two of my fingers as I spoke.

"Despite all that, I know he was really important to me. Whenever I hit some point in my life where I feel like throwing in the towel and giving up, thinking about him helps me keep going. Whenever I try to picture him, it's like I can hear him say to me, 'don't give up.'"

I picked the pen back up in my left hand. "I'm sorry," I said.

"I sound like a crazy lady, don't I?"

The boy shook his head. "It's a nice story," he said. "I'm sure that person would love to hear something like that."

"I'd like to think so," I said wryly.

I looked into the boy's emerald green eyes.

"Okay," I said. "Who am I making this out to?"

The boy smiled.

"Please make it out to Weiss Bennet," he said.

ABOUT THE AUTHOR:

Michael Emond is a writer born and raised in Northeast Ohio. Having always been passionate about storytelling in its various forms, Michael developed an interest in writing to better understand himself and the world around him.